Your
Friend

by

Steven Dale

Dedicated to my daughters
Michelle and Natalie

To,
 Kate

Hope you enjoy my book

Best wishes

Steven Wala

About the Author

Steven Dale has been happily married for 42 years. He has two daughters, three granddaughters and a crazy dog named Bella. He comes from Port Talbot in South Wales but now resides in Alicante, Spain.

Other books by Steven Dale
The Old Tin Box

Children's Books
The Planet Mirth Adventures One
The Planet Mirth Adventures Two
The Planet Stupiter

Chapter 1

Bourton on the Water

01st November 2019

Sean MacCarthy walked past the ubiquitous honey-coloured stone houses that straddled the River Windrush and thought back to his Uncle Sean's funeral.

His namesake was well thought of in the village because of his charitable work and willingness to help others. This showed in the volume of people that turned up to pay their respects.

He'd been a bachelor with no family of his own, eventually succumbing to his battle against cancer, leaving his entire estate to Sean's parents. It included the house in Pockhill Lane which they'd recently moved into.

Sean had spent a lot of time with his uncle, especially during the school holidays. He remembered one day in particular. It was a Bank Holiday Monday in August, and they'd gone to play football in the River Windrush. His uncle was too old to play, so he'd stood on the bank shouting words of encouragement.

It had been a tradition for almost a hundred years to play football in the ankle-deep water. The entire village turned out to watch, along with the tourists who'd seen nothing like it.

Later on, they went to 'The Mousetrap Inn'

with the rest of the players where they had a quiz to raise money for the local football teams.

As he got older, he began to look more like his uncle. They were both five foot seven and had the red hair that was inherent in the family, a sign of their Irish heritage. His father, Brendan, also had red hair but was slightly taller.

As he crossed over one of the low bridges, trailing his small piece of hand luggage behind him, he glanced over at the myriad tea rooms and shops. He couldn't believe how busy they were for a cold November day.

A few minutes later, he arrived at Pockhill Lane. His dad was outside, raking together the dead leaves from an ancient oak tree that stood like a sentinel in the garden. A stack of household rubbish had been piled together in the corner, awaiting clearance.

"Hi, Dad."

"Ah, Sean! I wasn't expecting you until later. How was the journey?"

"Fine. The bus was on time for a change. How have you been coping?"

"It's been hard, especially going through Sean's stuff and deciding what to throw out. There are some things in the attic he wanted you to have."

"What things?"

"There's a wooden trunk up there with birth certificates and documents going back generations. He wanted you to have it. He said it was a part of our history."

"That's a coincidence. I've been trying to do our family tree online. I didn't have enough to go on, so I gave up on it. I'll have a look later and see what's up there. Where's Mam?"

"She's in the kitchen making dinner. Let's go in and have a cuppa and a chat."

Brendan sat down in the porch to take off his gardening boots. He didn't want to incur the wrath of his wife.

Sean entered the house and felt immediately at ease. A wood-burning fire burned brightly in the Inglenook fireplace, creating warmth and atmosphere. The original exposed beams hugged the ceiling like an old friend and blended in perfectly with the stone walls.

The house had been renovated a few years earlier using skilled local craftsmen. They'd managed to retain many of the original features including the stone mullioned windows.

His mother, Sylvia, screamed with delight when she saw him, squeezing him within an inch of his life.

"Welcome home, Son. Sit down and I'll make us a nice cup of tea. How are things in London? Are you managing all right?" she asked.

"I'm fine, Mum. Up to my eyes in debt, but I'll pay it off once I start work."

Sean was sharing a flat with two other students near Kings College London. He was in his final year studying for a PhD in creative writing and enjoying every minute of it. He hoped to become a successful author one day.

Brendan walked in, minus his boots, and joined his son at the dining table. Sylvia placed a pot of hot tea and all the accoutrements in front of them.

"Dinner will be ready in an hour," she said.

"Thanks, Mam. I only had a light breakfast this morning, so I'm starving. Do you need a hand with anything in the garden, Dad?"

"Not until tomorrow. I've got a mini skip coming. You can help me fill it if you like."

"No problem."

"Did your father tell you about the trunk in the attic?" asked Sylvia.

"Yes, Mum. Once I've finished my tea, I'll go up and have a look."

"Why not? There's no time like the present," said his father.

After his tea, he went up to the room he used to stay in as a child and placed his case on the single bed. Little had changed over the years. A big antique mahogany wardrobe took up most of one wall, and a matching dresser stood between the two windows overlooking the garden.

He unpacked his laptop, had a quick freshen up in the hallway bathroom, and headed for the attic entrance.

The trapdoor in the ceiling was outside his parent's bedroom. He found a pole with a hook on the end leaning against the wall and used it to open the hatch. He pulled the sliding staircase down and walked up tentatively.

His imagination ran wild. He was thinking of old horror films and attics full of cobwebs and spiders. He couldn't have been more wrong. The whole area was spotless and even had a dormer window that allowed natural light to flood in. He knew his uncle was an organised person, but he didn't expect this. A comfy chair was placed strategically in front of the window where his uncle had probably spent hours reading. A row of metal filing cabinets stretched across one wall, full of paperwork going back decades.

He found the trunk hidden away in a corner, so he dragged it into the middle of the room to make the most of the light. The leather strips covering it were cracking in places, and the brass fittings were discoloured due to oxidisation, but despite that, it looked remarkably good. On the front edge of the case were the initials SM.

He opened it, and the smell of mildew wafted up his nostrils from the ancient yellowed documents within. He picked up a brown envelope and found his grandparent's birth certificates inside. He studied them for a while and realised they included his great grandparent's names and occupations. *That's just what I need to build my family tree,* he thought.

He organised the certificates into inverse chronological order, so he could add them to the website later.

After an hour of sifting through documents,

he'd gone back to the early 19th century with Sean MacCarthy being head of the family on each occasion.

The last birth certificate he picked up was for his five-times great grandfather, Sean MacCarthy, born in Skibbereen near Cork in 1825. It was attached to his last Will and Testament.

It bequeathed a substantial property in Ireland to his two surviving children. He placed the will on top of the birth certificates and continued searching.

Near the bottom, he found three books that looked old and tattered. The first one was entitled 'Mrs Beeton's Book of Household Management.' He set it to one side for his mother to read. She loved her cookery books.

The second one, 'The Boy's Book of Railways,' he placed back in the trunk.

The third one, which was blue and faded, had him mesmerised. There was no title or any clue as to its contents. He opened it carefully, its earthy fragrance invading his senses.

The first page caught him by surprise. His name was written across the top of the page in the most amazing penmanship. The words flowed across the page like wheat blowing in the wind.

"Sean! You'd better come down! Food will be served in a few minutes!" yelled his mother from downstairs.

"Okay! I'm on my way!" he yelled back.

He closed the book in disbelief and took it

downstairs along with the cookery book. He left the other documents there for later.

His father was sitting in his favourite armchair, watching the news.

"Did you find anything of interest, son?" he asked.

"You wouldn't believe it, Dad. I found loads of documents up there, but this is unbelievable," he said, waving the book around.

"What is it?"

"It's a story written by my five-times great grandfather, Sean MacCarthy. It's based on his life back in the 19th century. The penmanship is amazing."

"Wow! I didn't expect that. Your uncle never mentioned it."

"Perhaps he never knew it was there," said Sylvia, from the kitchen.

"As soon as I've eaten, I'm going back upstairs to read it. It's piqued my curiosity, to say the least.

I found something for you too, Mum. Mrs Beeton's Book on Household Management."

"Oh! I nearly bought one of those recently. It was in an antique shop in Broadway. Mrs Beeton was famous in her day, and nearly every household had one."

After his meal, Sean went up to his room, made himself comfortable and began to read.

Chapter 2

Sean MacCarthy – born 1825–
Skibbereen

The story you are about to read is true
and based on the fastidious journals that
I've kept since I was a young man.

My story begins on the 25th of September in the year of our Lord 1841. A day my family and I will have etched on our memories forever.

It was dawn, and a golden sun peeked its head above the horizon, announcing a brand new day. Dew clung to the ground like a moist blanket, and an eerie silence filled the air, disturbed only by the clatter of wheels and the clip-clopping of hooves.

Doctor O' Grady, a wizened old man with bushy eyebrows, arrived at our single-roomed mud hut made of turf and reined in the horses.

As he climbed down, he heard a panic-stricken voice radiating from within, filling him with dread.

"Mammy! Wake up! It's Rebecca! She's not breathing!" yelled my brother, Patrick, anxiously shaking my mother's arm.

She sprang up out of her straw bed, using my brother's arm for support. In one stride, she was at her baby's side.

Our father, Tom, followed close behind, falling over the chickens in his haste to get to her.

Our mother, Rose, held our baby sister in her arms and wailed. A sorrowful cry emanating from deep within her body. My father stretched out a calloused hand and stroked Rebecca's head as a solitary tear rolled down his cheek.

Patrick and I, aged just seventeen and sixteen respectively, were in tears ourselves, but we had our three younger sisters to think of who wept uncontrollably in the corner. We held them close and offered words of comfort.

The doctor entered our meagre home and placed his black bag on the floor alongside the small peat fire that smouldered in the corner. Smoke spiralled upwards, escaping through a small hole in the straw roof.

Like any other Catholic family of the time, we lived in subsistence, sharing our home with our livestock. We slept on straw, laid out in bundles on the bare floor. A blanket was a luxury we couldn't afford. Any incentive to improve our conditions was discouraged. Our landlord would simply increase the rent.

We were tenant farmers and lived in a small community known as a clachan, situated on the outskirts of Skibbereen, in the County of Cork, two miles from St. Patrick's Cathedral.

Skibbereen or Skibb, as it is better known, is thought to have derived from the word 'Skiff', a type of boat. Our town owes its origins to a raid of Algerian Pirates on the coastal town of Baltimore in 1630 when one hundred people were taken as white slaves. The survivors moved up the River Llen and established our town.

The doctor looked at my mother and the baby that lay lifeless in her arms.

"I'm sorry for your loss, Mrs MacCarthy. There was never much hope considering her size. Not many survive the fever," he said.

"But that's all we've got, Doctor. Hope for a better life for our children. Take that away, and we've got nothing," replied my father, emotionally.

"I understand, Tom. I can take her to St. Patrick's for you in the buggy if you wish. Father Sullivan will take care of her and organise the funeral. I can call in tomorrow and let you know the arrangements."

"Thank you, Doctor. We appreciate it."

He climbed aboard the buggy and held his hands out to our mother who held Rebecca close to her in a vice-like grip. With some encouragement from my father, she handed her over, then collapsed onto her knees, wailing pitifully.

The doctor placed Rebecca in a small box under his feet and covered her with a rag.

"My condolences to you all. I'll let the neighbours know," he said.

The two horses trotted off leaving a trail of steam and sweat behind. My father helped my mother up from the floor and coaxed her into the house.

News of our loss spread through the clachan like wildfire. Within the hour, our nearest neighbour, Patricia Ryan, arrived with her three children. Pat and my mother were very close friends and were always there to support each other in times of need.

Others arrived, and before we knew it, our little house was full.

My brother and I stood outside with our father, greeting people and thanking them for their support. When the last of them had been and gone, my father took us to one side.

"Your sister's passing doesn't change a thing, boys. In fact, it's all the more reason to stick to your plans. If you want a better life for yourselves, you'll have to emigrate because you won't find it here. You're both literate, thanks to your mother, so the world's your oyster."

"Maybe another year, and we'll have enough for the fare," I replied.

My brother and I had been lucky over the past few years, and we'd saved some money. The Union Workhouse had been built a mile to the North of Skibbereen, big enough to accommodate 800 inmates, and we'd found work there. The job eventually ended, and the building received its first admissions at the beginning of March.

"Keep working hard and you'll do it. I'll ask around and see if I can find more work for you. If you stay here any longer, you'll end up married with families of your own, like most of your friends. Have you decided where yet?"

"America, we think. New York or Boston," said Patrick.

"What about Argentina? A lot of Irish are moving there," said my father.

"We have thought about it, but there are too many unknowns. A steamer left for Argentina this morning from Dublin," I said.

"Whatever you choose, your mother and I will help you as much as we can."

"Are we harvesting in the morning, Da?" I

asked.

"Yes, bright and early."

"Everything is ready. We prepared the pits yesterday," said Patrick.

A feeling of despair hung over us that evening. My mother was inconsolable and cried for most of the night, eventually falling asleep in my father's arms.

26ᵗʰ September 1841

We woke the following morning at first light. My mother and ten-year-old sister, Cathy, were already up making the usual breakfast of potato, oatmeal and skimmed milk. My younger sisters, Claire and Mary, aged eight and six respectively, were still fast asleep.

It was a lot of work preparing food. Most men could eat up to 14lbs of potatoes a day, the women a lot less.

The white potatoes, or lumpers as we called them, were our main source of sustenance and produced a high yield that could grow abundantly in less favourable soil.

After breakfast, we left the cabin mentally prepared for a hard day's work. We put our boots on outside and crossed the dirt track road to the fields beyond.

The rest of the clachan were in a buoyant mood. The summer weather had been perfect, and we were all expecting a bumper crop. We'd survived the difficult months of July and August when food was scarce and now looked forward to less hungry times.

My brother looked out at the raised beds before him that ran in perfect parallel lines across the whole acreage. He raised his arms above his head and stretched his six-foot two-inch frame. He was the image of my father, and he'd inherited his piercing blue eyes and red hair. One time he'd even considered a career as a prizefighter. Our mother was horrified: *you'll achieve far more by using your brains rather than your fists,* she would say when the subject was raised.

Our father had taught us both how to box at an early age. *A man must learn how to defend himself,* he would say as he put us through our paces.

I'm a mixture of both my parents. I've my mother's green eyes and my father's red hair. I'm smaller in stature compared to my brother, standing at five foot seven.

"Well, at least the weather's good," said my father as we began our work.

"Let's hope it stays that way," I replied.

A few minutes later, I heard the sound of horses. It was Doctor O' Grady with news of the funeral. We carried on working. We had a lot to do in a short space of time.

Two acres of the harvest had to be stored in pits to feed us and our pig for the next 9 to 10 months. Some we stored as seed potatoes for the following year. The rest would be collected by our landlord as rent, fodder for his livestock and food for his staff.

The girls joined us later, after completing their chores in the house. They'd been busy scrubbing our spare set of clothes in readiness for the funeral.

At midday, my mother rang the bell that hung outside the hut, summoning us in for dinner.

"Thank God for that. I'm famished," said Patrick, laying down his spade.

We took our boots off outside, entered, and sat around the table with the rest of the family.

"Doctor O' Grady said the funeral is set for 10 am tomorrow. There'll be another one at the same time, a businessman from Baltimore. Father Sullivan said there would be no charge and not to worry, he's taking care of everything."

"He's a good man. I'll thank him when I see him," replied my father.

"Make sure you clean your boots tonight after work. I've clean clothes ready for you all. We may be poor, but I want us looking as presentable as possible," said my mother.

We all nodded in agreement and tucked into our food. When we'd finished, we returned to work feeling recharged.

We were pulling on our boots when we saw a coach in the distance, heading our way.

"That'll be old man Charles after his potatoes," said my father.

"Tough. He'll have to wait. We'll be a couple of days yet," I replied.

Charles Smithers, our landlord, owned 500 acres of land in total. He kept his best pasture land to raise livestock to feed the ever-growing demand for beef in Britain while Catholic families like us had to farm smaller plots of marginal land.

His only son, George, and his daughter-in-law, Bridget, had both died of tuberculosis, leaving him to look after his only grandson, Charles Junior, who would eventually inherit the estate.

None of us had ever met the grandson, and we didn't particularly want to. His reputation as a philanderer and hoodwinker preceded him.

He was a major headache for his grandfather, who sent him to America to expand the family business. He hoped against hope that the young man would change his compulsive ways and become a responsible adult.

The coach, led by a team of four horses, pulled up alongside us. Charles opened the door and stepped out, looking delicate and frail. His 75 years did nothing to improve his demeanour. He growled at my father in his usual manner.

"Where are my potatoes, Tom?"

"In the ground, where else would they be," replied Patrick, under his breath.

"We'll have them ready for you in a week. We lost our daughter yesterday, so we're a bit behind," replied my father.

"Not my problem. My men will be here in 5 days to collect them."

"Have some empathy, Charles. We've just lost

a child," said my father, his temper rising.

"Empathy won't feed my livestock. Five days Tom and not a day longer."

The coach left in a cloud of dust leaving my father in a perturbed state.

"Bastard. That man's got no humanity," he said.

"Don't worry, Da. We'll manage. The girls will have to help," I said positively.

We continued to work until the light began to fade then returned to the hut feeling exhausted. Patrick and I cleaned the boots while our father lit the peat fire. My mother and the girls prepared supper while I composed a letter to my esteemed friend and author, Boz.

I came into contact with him through Father Sullivan. We'd never met in person, but we'd been in touch by letter since I was a young lad. He's the reason this story exists. He inspired me to keep a journal so that one day I could write something to pass on to future generations.

Boz was becoming more and more successful as an author. His latest work was published in instalments in a magazine called Bentley's Miscellany, and thanks to Father Sullivan, and the church network, I was able to obtain copies.

After supper, we all collapsed onto our straw beds, too tired to talk. Within minutes, we were fast asleep.

Chapter 3

27th September 1841

The following morning we were up bright and early. We had our normal breakfast and set off on the hour-long walk to St. Patrick's. A cold northerly wind blew, hinting at the bitter onslaught of winter. The girls pulled their tattered shawl's tighter around their bodies and huddled together for warmth.

"A brisk pace, and we'll soon warm up," said my father lengthening his stride. "There'll be no work today regardless of what Charles Smithers may have to say. The lumpers will be ready when they're ready."

"Can Sean and I go for a walk around Skibb after the funeral, Da? We haven't been for a while," asked Patrick.

"I don't see why not? I'll probably go there myself for a quick drink."

"I'll take the girl's home. I want to get food ready for tomorrow so we can concentrate on the harvest," said my mother.

Halfway into our journey, having all warmed up, we stopped at the entrance to our landlord's property, the Manor House or what the locals referred to as the Big House.

The residence looked amazing with its fifteen bedrooms and Georgian architecture. Cows grazed contentedly off the lush fertile grass.

"To think that our ancestors once owned all this leaves a dull ache in my heart. We'll never be allowed to own a property in my lifetime," said my father.

"Never say never," I said.

"What do you mean, Son?"

"It's something I read in a book by my friend Boz. It means nothing is impossible, anything can happen."

We all knew the history of the MacCarthy family and how our land had been confiscated by the English crown during the turbulent 16th and 17th centuries. It had been handed over to people with British and Protestant identity, totally changing the lives of the MacCarthy's forever.

"We'd better crack on. I want to get there early, so I can thank Father Sullivan for all his help," said my father.

We passed a few farms on the way and were offered words of sympathy from our neighbours.

As we walked over Clover Hill, we could see St Patrick's in the distance. The t-shaped church with its galleried transepts, built in 1826 in the neoclassical design, looked magnificent as we approached North Street.

Nearby, stood the Court House, an imposing building of cut limestone designed by the Cork architect, George Pain.

The heavenly scent of freshly cut grass filled the air, and the melodic sound of the River Llen played in our ears as it meandered onwards towards the sea, some twelve kilometres away.

Father Sullivan stood outside waiting to greet us.

"I'm sorry for your loss," he said.

"Thank you, and thanks for everything you've done," replied my father.

"Your welcome, Tom. Come inside and warm up. It's a cold wind today."

"Who's the other funeral for?" asked my father.

"A Mr John White who's family own land in Baltimore. He was born in Skibbereen and wanted to be buried here in the family crypt. Here's his son now," he replied.

"Francis, this is Tom. It's his daughter Rebecca's funeral today."

"Nice to meet you, Tom. I wish it was under better circumstances. No man should have to bury his child."

"My condolences for your loss," my father replied.

We entered the church and sat down at the back where seats had been reserved for us. A few of our neighbours were there and whispered words of sympathy across the aisles.

We all looked a bit bedraggled compared to the refinery of the White family who sat bleary-eyed at the front.

My father clenched my mother's hand tightly as she wept while my brother and I comforted our sisters.

"It doesn't matter whether you're rich or poor.

Losing a loved one is just as painful," I said, philosophically.

Patrick nodded in agreement as the priest began.

After the service, both coffins were carried to the cemetery. Six men carried Mr White's while my father managed Rebecca's on his own.

Once outside, Francis approached the priest and said: "see to the child first. It's what my father would have done."

We all nodded in appreciation and continued to the graveside.

My father got there first and looked down at the small wooden cross crudely inscribed with her name. That was the moment it hit him. Until then, he'd remained strong for us all, holding his emotions in, but that cross was too much to bear, and he cried uncontrollably.

My brother and I took the coffin off him and lowered it into the grave.

Father Sullivan held another small service over the tiny coffin while the rest of us stood around in prayer.

When both funerals were over, Francis White approached us and spoke to my father.

"We've been having a wake at the Becher Arms Hotel in town. Feel free to join us."

"Thank you. I think I will. I normally go there when I'm in town."

"Mention my name to the proprietor, and she'll take care of you. We have a private room booked there."

"I know the owner well. She's a friend of my wife's. They both worked together as maids at the Manor House."

We walked together as a family for a short distance, then went our separate ways. My mother took the girl's home while we headed into town feeling emotionally drained.

The streets of Skibbereen were alive with activity. It was market day, and the stalls selling linen, wool and agricultural products were thriving, despite their products being substandard. The best of their labours were sent to the English Market in Cork for the wealthier clients or exported to Britain.

People from the surrounding towns and villages had merged on the town for the day. Barefooted children in rags played on the streets while shabbily dressed gentlemen waited around patiently for the mail to arrive from Cork.

We passed an eclectic mixture of properties from small thatched cottages to more refined buildings that displayed the varying degrees of wealth in the town. The side streets leading off led down to the quays and stores on the River Llen. In the distance, on Windmill Hill, we could see the high walls of the Union Workhouse, a constant reminder of how precarious our lives were.

As we passed the apothecary, Mr Crowley, the owner, came out and offered his condolences. We thanked him and continued on our way, not trusting ourselves to talk about it without breaking into tears.

We arrived at the Becher Arms Hotel amidst a throng of people. The mail coach had just arrived, its wheels caked with mud. An enterprising young boy had set up a shoeshine outside and was doing a roaring trade. The crowd gathered around, jostling for position, hoping for news from afar.

The inside of the hotel was nothing like I imagined. Dark oak beams stretched across the ceiling, and the air was infused with the smell of whisky. A riotous crowd gathered around the coffee bar, debating and arguing the politics of the day while a toothless barmaid served them with a gummy smile.

The proprietor, Mrs Mary Hegarty, who'd been running the place for several years, beckoned to my father from across the room. We headed towards her, our feet sticking to the floorboards as we walked.

"I'm so sorry for your loss, Tom. Rose must be devastated," she said.

"Yes, she is, but what can you do?"

"Can I get you something, a drink or some food?"

"I believe you're holding a wake here for a Mr John White? His son invited us."

"Yes, we are. They've been using the back room. There's cold food laid out in there if you want to go through."

"We will. Thanks, Mary."

As we walked through, my father and I heard a familiar voice. It was Charles Smithers, our landlord. He was sitting in the corner deep in conversation with a gentleman dressed in an expensive tweed suit.

"Fuck him and his potatoes," said my father, under his breath.

A shiver ran down my spine when I entered the room. A large oak table lay bare in the centre where the coffin would have been. Although the White's were a Christian family, they had followed some pagan rituals. The mirror on the wall had been turned to face the other way, and the clock had been stopped. Clay pipes, tobacco and snuff, were available as the male's in the family were expected to take a puff to ward off evil spirits.

Despite the depressing surroundings, I knew there'd been a lot of merriment in this room over the last few days. There had probably been copious amounts of alcohol consumed by the family, which explained the bleary eyes I'd witnessed at the church.

We were standing by the small bar when the White's arrived. Francis and his wife joined us and poured five good measures of whisky, handing one to each of us.

"Is it all right if the boys have a drink?" he asked.

"Yes, as long as you don't tell their mother."

"Good. Then we'll have a toast: **Death leaves a heartache no one can heal. Love leaves a memory**

no one can steal."

We all raised our glasses and drank the whisky down in one go.

It wasn't long before a fiddler appeared, playing sorrowful tunes at first, which soon became more raucous as the whisky flowed. Mary brought in some plates of trout, and Kerry mutton with potatoes, a rare treat for us. I couldn't remember the last time I'd eaten meat apart from the odd rabbit we'd caught. Before long, a party ensued celebrating the life of John White.

An hour later, I asked my father if Patrick and I could go for a wander around town.

"Yes, but be careful. There's a lot of rabble about on market day. Stay out of trouble, and I'll meet you back here at six. If I'm not outside, come into the bar and drag me out."

We both nodded and left our father to drown his sorrows.

Chapter 4

We arrived at the market square to an ocean of people. Loud voices could be heard, people paying for goods and bartering. Traders haggled with everyone, regardless of wealth, trying to get the best price for their wares.

A gang of children were standing on a low wall, laughing hysterically as a local farmer ran through the stalls in pursuit of an escaped pig. It culminated in the farmer falling flat on his face in a puddle of mud.

Young girls from neighbouring towns flirted unabashedly with us, but we both tried to appear aloof, secretly enjoying the attention.

When we got to the town hall, we sat on the steps outside to take in the ambience. My brother spoke to Tim O'Brien, a friend who lived in our clachan. He looked older than my brother even though they were the same age. Maybe it was the fact that he was married with a young family that had aged him so prematurely.

My eyes lit up when Mr Crowley from the apothecary passed by and handed me a newspaper.

"I've been keeping this for you, Sean. It's a new one that's just been launched, and it's called The Cork Examiner. Someone left it behind, so I kept it for you," he said.

"Thanks a million, Mr Crowley. I really appreciate it," I said.

The time passed quickly for us both. I read the

paper from back to front while Patrick spoke to nearly everyone that passed.

"Anything interesting in there?" asked my brother.

"There's a fascinating article in there about the history of Liverpool and the dock area. It says the living conditions there are worse than anywhere in England, despite the job opportunities.

Brunel is going to build a new steamship made entirely of iron, and it's going to have a screw propeller, whatever that is."

"There's no stopping that man. He's going to change the face of the world as we know it," said Patrick.

At five o'clock, the market stalls closed, and the crowds diminished, so we headed back to the hotel.

When we got to the alleyway that ran alongside it, I heard a faint cry for help and what sounded like groaning.

"Did you hear that, Pat? Sounds like someone's in a bit of bother."

"I heard it, but we've been told to stay out of trouble."

"We can't ignore it. What if someone gets murdered? It'll be on our conscience forever."

"On your head be it," said Patrick.

We walked warily down the narrow lane, listening attentively for any signs of danger. As we neared the quayside, we could see a gentleman in his late fifties, wearing a tweed suit, being set upon by two ruffians.

"He was in the bar earlier talking to Charles Smithers," I said.

One of the antagonists had long dark hair tied up in a ponytail and an ugly scar on his face. He held the gentleman firmly by the arms while his partner in crime, who was totally bald, continuously punched him in the stomach.

"You should have given us your wallet when we asked!" yelled Scarface.

"I hate you rich bastard's! You think you're better than us!" screamed the bald one while he continued to lay into him with his fists.

Fishermen were sitting along the pier, repairing their nets, impervious to the man's plight. Passersby continued walking, ignoring the fracas, not wishing to get involved.

"All that is necessary for the triumph of evil is that good men do nothing," I said, quoting the Irish political philosopher, Edmund Burke.

"Never a truer word was spoken," replied my brother, rolling up his sleeves.

"Keep on walking boys! This is none of your business!" yelled Scarface.

"We're making it our business," replied Patrick calmly.

The bald one turned, looked us both up and down and laughed.

"Piss off, the pair of you. Young boys like you should be getting ready for bed," he said.

"If you give him his wallet back and walk away, I promise we won't hurt you," said Patrick, looking him squarely in the eye.

He laughed even more. "I've got underpants older than you two. Now piss off while you can still walk," he said.

"I thought so, Baldy. I could smell them from the market square," I said, sounding bolder than I felt.

They let go of the gentleman and concentrated their efforts on us.

The bald one reacted first and ran towards Patrick with his fists flying. Scarface ran towards me, snarling like a wild dog, spittle flying from his mouth.

We both stood our ground and assumed a pugilist's stance, as our father had taught us. Patrick ducked under a swinging right and caught the bald guy with an uppercut. It landed perfectly, and the guy just collapsed to the floor unconscious.

I took a little longer, dancing and weaving like a ballerina. I didn't have the knockout punch like my brother, but I was quicker on my feet. Despite several attempts, Scarface couldn't get near me. After ten minutes of punching fresh air, he gave up and collapsed to the floor, puffing and panting.

"What took you so long?" asked my brother, laughing hysterically.

"I didn't want to get blood on my clothes. They're clean."

Patrick patted me on the back as we walked over to the man in the tweed suit who lay groaning on the floor. A walking stick lay beside him, evidence of a disability. He held a crimson-stained handkerchief to his nose that was bleeding profusely. I helped him to his feet and handed him his stick.

"Are you all right?" I asked.

"Yes, I'm fine. A bit of damage to my pride, but I'll survive. How can I ever thank you?"

"No need for that. We were just doing the right thing. Come to the hotel, and we'll get you cleaned up," said Patrick.

"Thank you very much, gentlemen. You wouldn't believe how many people walked past and ignored what was going on. What are your names?"

"I'm Patrick MacCarthy, and this is my brother Sean."

"Ebenezer Foley, at your service. I'll be forever in your debt," he said, shaking our hands.

We entered the hotel bar, and silence fell over the room. Everyone turned to look at the bloodied face of Ebenezer. Mary ran from behind the bar whilst ordering her barmaid to bring a bowl of water and some linen. She sat him down in the corner and checked him over.

"No broken bones by the look of it, but you'll be aching tomorrow. What happened?" she asked.

"Two ruffians set upon me, looking for a quick shilling. These two fine young gentlemen who are a credit to the human race rescued me."

My father entered the room looking slightly drunk.

"What have you two been up to?" he slurred.

Patrick gave him a blow by blow account, then introduced Ebenezer.

"You were in here earlier talking to Charles Smithers. He's our landlord," said my father.

"Don't remind me. What a cantankerous man. I'm a director of the Cork Steam Packet Company, and he wanted to export some goods to America, but I'm not doing business with the likes of him. I hope he's not a friend of yours."

"There's no love lost between us," replied my father.

"I met his grandson in Boston. He's not a popular person, a chip off the old block, you might say. He won a saloon in a card game, but it wouldn't surprise me if he cheated. The man is a ruthless charlatan with a Machiavellian approach to life. I'd give him a wide berth if your paths ever cross."

"We're hoping to go to America one day if we can save enough for the fare. Maybe next year with a bit of luck," said Patrick.

"I can help you with that. It's the least I can do considering what you've done for me. In fact, you'd be doing me a favour."

"What do you mean?" I asked.

"I've been looking to employ a couple of trustworthy lads like yourselves to look after the security of our cargo in Boston. It will be a permanent position. I don't trust the security company I use now because some of our stock has gone missing. Whoever is responsible has been very clever about it. It's not a great discrepancy, but over the space of a year, it all adds up."

"When would we be leaving?" asked Patrick.

"You'd sail on the SS Sirius on the 13th December, bound for Liverpool where you'd spend Christmas. On the 03rd January, you'd sail on the SS Britannia, bound for Boston. There'll be a short stop in Halifax on the way to drop off the mail.

The job includes a stipend, of course, and all your travelling expenses would be borne by the company. I'll probably join you later on in the year, but for now, my presence is required here."

"We accept your offer, Mr Foley," said Patrick.

"Yes, It sounds perfect, and the 03rd of January is my eighteenth birthday," I said.

"If I was you, I'd learn as much about Boston as I could. It's steeped in history, and a little knowledge would go a long way. I have some books at home you could borrow. You could read them on your journey.

It would be a good idea if you stayed at my home in Cork on the 11th of December, two nights before you sail. It'll give us time to sort you out with some suitable attire that befits an employee of our company. I own a drapery and menswear store on St Patrick's Street, so I can sort that out for you."

"I can't believe it. I never thought something like this could happen to us," I said.

"Never say never," said my father, winking at me.

"I'll have my carriage pick you up at 09.00 am on the 11th of December. If you're on Charles Smithers's land, my coachman will find you," said Ebenezer.

"Your carriage is here, Mr Foley!" yelled the toothless barmaid.

We made our way outside and waved him off. As we were about to start our long walk home, Mary handed my father a parcel.

"Give this to Rose and the girls. It's just some ham and cheese leftover from the wake," she said.

"Thank you, Mary. They'll be delighted," replied my father.

My father swayed as we walked down North Street.

"The fresh air is mixing with the alcohol. My legs have got a mind of their own," he slurred.

I took the food off him in case he dropped it. He then looked up at the sky and said, "Maybe Rebecca is up there, looking out for us."

My brother and I both nodded in agreement. It had certainly been a day to remember, full of sadness and elation.

The walk home took longer than we expected due to our father's constant need to empty his bladder. We sang for most of the way and arrived home as the sun was setting.

My mother took one look at him, shook her head in mock disgust and laughed.

"It's been a long time since I've seen your father like that. What have you got there?"

"Some leftovers off Mary at the Becher Arms," I replied.

Cathy, Claire and Mary were sitting in the corner amongst the straw. At the mention of food, they flew to the dining table.

"Can we have some now?" asked Cathy.

An opportunity to eat something other than potatoes was a rarity in our home.

"Of course," said my mother. "What about you, boys? Are you hungry?"

"No thank you, Ma. We're fine," we replied.

She turned to ask my father, but he'd collapsed onto his bed of straw and was snoring like a pig.

While my mother and sisters ate, we recapitulated the events of the day. Our mother sat there with her mouth agape.

"You could have been killed! What if they had a weapon?" she yelled.

"We couldn't ignore it. We'd be as bad as everyone else," replied Patrick.

"So, you'll be leaving us in December then," said my mother, with a heavy heart.

"Yes, we will," I replied.

"It will be for the best. If you want something other than a life of poverty and potatoes, then you'll have to leave. Maybe the girls can join you when they're older."

"Of course, Ma. If that's what they want," said my brother.

Before we went to sleep that night, we all said a prayer for our sister, apart from our father who was sleeping contentedly in the corner.

Chapter 5

11th December 1841

December couldn't come quickly enough for my brother and me. For the last few months, we'd kept busy by bringing in the harvest and preparing things for the following year.

Charles Smithers had called for his share of the crop, and Father Sullivan dropped by occasionally to check on our mother who'd been in a state of melancholy since the death of our sister.

I gave Father Sullivan a letter to send to Boz. I wrote about the events in Skibbereen, how we met Ebenezer and our plans to emigrate to America on my eighteenth birthday.

During the night's, Patrick and I sat outside our home until the early hours, planning and discussing the future. Sleep had remained elusive to the pair of us.

The day finally arrived. An elegant carriage, drawn by two fine horses, pulled up outside our door. It was earlier than expected because of the fair weather. The driver, a pleasant enough chap with a penchant for whistling non-existent tunes, hopped down and introduced himself.

"Eugene, at your service," he said.

"I'm Sean, and this is my brother Patrick. Thank you for picking us up," I said.

"It's all part of my job. I'm down this way often. My sister lives in Skibbereen."

My father and sisters looked at the carriage in amazement. They'd never seen such refinement. The interior seats were made of quality black leather, the same colour as the rest of the equipage.

Suddenly, my father laughed.

"What's tickled you?" I asked.

"What are people going to think when they see you arriving in Cork? Two men dressed in rags climbing out of a gentleman's carriage; they'll be baffled."

Our mother joined in the laughter and hugged us both tightly.

"Don't forget to write. Send your mail to Father Sullivan at St. Patrick's. He'll make sure I receive it," she said.

"We will, Ma," replied Patrick.

"Look out for each other, and choose your friends wisely," said our father.

We had no worldly possessions to take with us apart from my journal and a few tattered books. We climbed aboard, and the carriage pulled off while our three sisters ran behind, waving their arms frantically.

We sat in silence for a while, both lost in our own thoughts until my brother broke our reverie. He started laughing as he leaned his arm out of the window and attempted a rather lame impression of Queen Victoria by waving his hand at the workers in the fields.

However, our jollity and carefree mood soon turned to sadness when we were a mile or two past

Skibbereen. We witnessed a young Catholic family being evicted from their home. The mother held onto her five children, sobbing uncontrollably while her husband pleaded with the local constabulary for leniency.

We looked at each in mutual understanding. The threat of eviction hung over us all if the crops failed or something untoward happened. It reinforced our resolve to make things work in America and make our family proud.

The roads to Cork from the surrounding towns had been significantly improved over recent years, and the elliptical spring suspension made easy work of the journey.

I thought back to our last visit to Cork, two years ago. We'd gone as a family except for Claire and Mary, who'd stayed with our neighbours. The journey was deemed too arduous for their little legs to cope with.

We'd spent the night in Bandon with our late grandfather, then continued on to Cork, arriving the next day.

It had been my father's idea. He'd wanted us to see the newly built Church of Saint Mary's on Pope's Quay. It was one of the finest buildings we'd ever seen.

He took us on a tour of the City and pointed out famous landmarks and places of interest. His knowledge of the city knew no bounds, most of which had been passed on to him by our grandfather, who'd worked in Cork for most of his life.

My daydreams were broken when we stopped for sustenance and a change of horses. Before long, we were on our way again, arriving in Cork as the sun was setting.

We crossed the North Bridge over the River Lee and made our way down the tree-lined North Main Street. It was wider than most streets, allowing for two carriages to pass each other comfortably. The lamplighters were busy with their evening chores of lighting the gaslights. Commercial enterprises and Georgian houses bordered us on either side, and the hustle and bustle of everyday life was omnipresent.

The inner city was densely populated and composed of many Catholic families who'd moved there from the countryside in search of a better life and wages. What was once an affluent area had turned into a slum. Children ran around barefoot, and many wore rags like us.

"I don't think we've been to this part of the city before, Sean," said my brother.

"You're right. I didn't realise there was so much poverty in Cork. Father Sullivan told me that many of the wealthier merchants are moving to the outskirts. It makes sense now."

A few minutes later, we arrived at Foley's Drapery and Menswear in St Patrick's Street.

"They're expecting you, so don't worry. I'll wait outside until you're finished," said Eugene.

My brother and I walked into the shop

nervously, but an elderly rotund man with a jocular face soon put us at ease.

"Ah! The MacCarthy's! We've been expecting you," he said.

He looked us up and down as if we were two prized bulls.

"I need to measure you both for a full wardrobe that we'll deliver to the SS Sirius in readiness for your journey."

He ran his tape measure over every part of our body like a seasoned professional, then left the room.

"If any other man touched me there, I'd knock him out," said my brother.

"I thought you were enjoying it by the look on your face," I replied.

He returned a few minutes later with two suits. A young girl walked behind him carrying two long coats, two flat caps, shoes, scarves, gloves, socks and a full set of underwear.

"These will do to get you started. They're off the peg so they won't be an exact fit. The rest of your attire will be bespoke and sent to the SS Sirius. You can change into your clothes when you arrive at Mr Foley's."

Fifteen minutes later, we arrived at Ebenezer's house on the outskirts of the city. Eugene opened the ornate gates at the entrance then guided the carriage down the long and winding drive. It was a beautiful Georgian house, surrounded by trees and a resplendently manicured garden.

We stood outside, taking in its magnificence while Eugene rang the bell. Within seconds, an elderly gentleman opened the door and beckoned us in.

"Good day, gentlemen. Place your possessions on the stairs, and I'll take them up to your room. Mr Foley is waiting for you in his study with the rest of the family. Please follow me," he said.

He led us through a vast, opulent hallway. A chandelier hung from the ceiling, and magnificent paintings adorned the walls. Expensive silverware and fine porcelain were strategically placed on mahogany furniture.

Ebenezer, along with his wife and three children, stood up as we entered.

"Ah! my knights in shining armour!" said Ebenezer. "This is my wife, Anne, my oldest son John, my daughter Kathleen, and our youngest son George."

John was a few years older than us, while Kathleen looked about my age. The youngest looked about thirteen.

I just stood there entranced. I couldn't take my eyes of Kathleen, who was the most beautiful woman I'd ever seen. Her long blond hair and blue eyes were breathtaking, and her translucent skin shone like the sun.

We shook hands with them all, my hand lingering in Kathleen's slightly longer than necessary.

"Thank you so much for what you did for our

father. We'll be forever in your debt," she said, staring into my eyes.

"We were glad to help, and your father has repaid us in more ways than you can imagine," I replied.

An elderly lady entered the room carrying a tray of tea and cakes.

"Some refreshments after your long journey," she said.

"This is my housekeeper, Elsie. Her husband, William, you met at the door. They've been in service to our family for nearly forty years," said Ebenezer.

"Please to meet you, gentlemen," said Elsie. "Your room is ready, and there's a hot bath being prepared as we speak. Dinner will be served in an hour."

We drank our tea, then William escorted us to our room that was on the top floor of the three-storied house.

"My God, this room is bigger than our house in the clachan," said Patrick.

Two enormous beds stood side by side and red velvet curtains hung from ceiling to floor. Our clothes were laid out on the bed, along with a towel for each of us. My books had been stacked neatly between the beds.

We both smiled and looked at the hip bath.

"Who's going first?" I asked.

"You, I think," replied Patrick as he burst into song: *"If you want to be squeaky clean for your sweet Kathleen."*

"What do you mean?"

"I saw the way you were looking at her. Smitten at first glance. She's way out of your league brother. Rich Protestants don't mix with poor Catholics."

"I know, but one can always dream," I replied.

Believe it or not, it was the first proper bath we'd ever had. Up until then, it'd been a bowl of hot water, a sponge, or a dip in the river.

Within the hour, we were both dressed in our new suits and shiny shoes. The transformation was amazing, and we felt like millionaires.

We arrived downstairs, and William showed us to the dining room. They were all sitting around an enormous mahogany table. Crystal glasses and silver cutlery sparkled in the candlelight.

"I hope we haven't kept you waiting?" I said.

"No, we've only just sat down," replied Ebenezer.

It was one of those occasions when my brother and I felt grateful for all the tips our mother had given us about dining etiquette. As a young girl, she'd worked in service at the Big House and educated herself along the way.

Elsie and a young servant girl entered the room carrying bowls of vegetable soup. My stomach rumbled in anticipation as the smell drifted towards me. Ebenezer said a prayer, then we began.

Patrick and John were talking about my

brother's favourite subject, engineering. They spoke about its effects on industry and the innovative machines appearing on the market.

"I think trains are going to be the future. The Great Western Railway has been a wonderful success," said John.

"Brunel is an amazing man. Some of his ideas are ingenious," said Patrick.

"By the way, I've booked rooms for us at the Imperial Hotel in Cork for tomorrow night," said Ebenezer.

"Why?" I asked.

"I want you to meet a newly married couple who are staying there. They'll be travelling to America with you. I thought it would be nice if you got to know each other.

I own a drapery and menswear store in Boston, and they're going to manage it for me. The wife, Teresa, has run my drapery in Cork for the last five years. Her husband, James Ryan, is going to look after the financial side of things. He's an accountant.

James is an interesting character with an incredible memory. He was a professional poker player for many years and very successful, but he's given all that up now for a more respected occupation. Teresa refused to marry him unless he changed his lifestyle."

"I know the hotel. I've always wanted to stay there," I said.

My brother and I ate with gusto, and after the

second course of lamb and roast potatoes, we could eat no more. Our stomachs weren't used to that volume of food so, with reluctance, we refused the dessert.

Kathleen and I chatted like old friends, and her love for books paralleled mine.

"Would you like me to show you our library?" she asked.

"Yes, please," I replied.

"There are some books in there on the history of Boston. Can you give them to Sean?" said Ebenezer.

"Certainly, Father," she replied.

I'd never seen such an eclectic mixture of books in one place. She found what she was looking for and handed them to me.

"These should keep you busy for a while."

"Thank you. I'll read these over the coming weeks," I said.

She showed me her favourite books, some of which I'd read, and her face glowed with a passion.

"It's so nice to talk to someone who has such an avid interest in reading. It's a shame we won't be seeing more of each other in the future," I said.

"I wouldn't be so sure of that if I were you," she replied.

"What do you mean?"

"I'm going to Boston in March with my father, and I'll probably stay there for a few years.

A friend of ours has a farm in Concord. I'm going to work there and study their methods. I'd like to have my own farm here in Ireland one day."

"Have you worked on the farm before?"

"Yes, I've spent quite a few summers there over the years.

My father has a house opposite Boston Common. Maybe we could go for a walk around it one day. It's a beautiful place, full of history, but it has a dark side."

"I'm intrigued. What do you mean by a dark side?"

"I'll tell you more about it when we're there."

"I shall look forward to it."

We returned to the dining area and finished the night with a glass of brandy in front of the fireplace.

It had been a day of firsts for my brother and me. Our first proper bath, our first suit, our first meal with silver cutlery, and our first taste of brandy.

We retired that night and had our first sleep in a proper bed.

Chapter 6

12th December 1841

We woke the following morning feeling fresh and eager to face the day. After breakfast, we said our farewells and boarded the carriage.

The biggest surprise for me was when Kathleen shook my hand and whispered in my ear, "I'll be seeing you soon."

After a short journey, we arrived at the coach yard of the Imperial Hotel on Pembroke Street.

The Coachmaster welcomed us with much aplomb and ceremony, then escorted us to the entrance.

A small merchant ship was conveniently moored directly opposite us, and barrels were being rolled across the road, into the cellar. Throngs of people of all ages went about their business, some working, some begging and some seeking employment.

Shipbuilding, brewing, distilling, tanning and butter, were all thriving, but overpopulation still meant a shortage of jobs.

The lack of work made conditions hard for everyone, and the recently opened Workhouse was full to capacity.

I thought back to when I was a boy. I'd stood on this very spot with my grandfather who used to work here unloading the merchant ships.

He'd regale me stories about Cork and times

gone by. He told me about the Imperial and its history. How it had once been commercial rooms where the cities butter merchants would sit and discuss the business of the day. Irish butter has always been a much sought after commodity because of its longevity at sea.

A young architect, Thomas Deane, responsible for many of the fine buildings in Cork, was commissioned to extend the rooms to serve as a hotel for visitors, traders and merchants.

My grandfather would have been so proud to see us walking into that fine building, dressed in all our refinery.

"Once you've checked in, we'll meet in the bar. I've got some documents regarding your employment for you to sign, and I want to introduce you to James and Teresa," said Ebenezer.

It was another first for us when we were allocated individual rooms. After a quick look around, we headed for the bar.

Ebenezer made the introductions, and we all shook hands.

James was about an inch taller than me with jet black hair. He had a lean, sinewy frame, an intelligent face and black penetrating eyes that seemed to stare into your soul.

His wife, Teresa, reminded me of my mother. She had red hair, green eyes, a scattering of freckles on her face, and a charismatic personality that could fill a room.

"So, we'll be travelling together," I said.

"Yes, we will. It'll be a long tedious journey, but I'm sure we'll find something to keep us entertained," said James.

"As long as it's not poker," said his wife with a frown.

"My poker days are long gone, Dear," said James, sincerely.

Patrick read through our terms of employment which included a fair wage for the duration of our employment, travel expenses and accommodation in Liverpool and Boston.

"These are your wages for the next four weeks," said Ebenezer, handing each of us an envelope. "I've written to the Boston Bank and opened accounts for you. Your wages will be paid there every Thursday.

A room has been reserved for you at the Adelphi Hotel, in Liverpool, where you'll stay until your departure on the SS Britannia on the 03rd January."

I opened my envelope to find fifteen guineas within, which was far higher than the average wage at the time.

My brother and I put two guineas into an envelope and handed it back to Ebenezer. It was something we'd agreed upon earlier.

"Would you mind giving this to our parents if it's not too much trouble?" I asked.

"No problem. Eugene is down that way at least once a week, visiting his sister."

We both thanked him, signed the employment

contract and discussed a plan of action.

"As far as we can tell, there's no problem with our cargo when it leaves Cork and arrives in Liverpool. The discrepancies occur in Boston," said Ebenezer.

"Do you have a distribution warehouse there?" asked Patrick.

"Yes, and there's always someone on guard at any given time."

"I want to study the flow of goods from the cargo hold to the customer. Somebody has found a way of cheating the system. Once we get there, we'll have a better idea," I said.

"Would you be interested in setting up your own security company? I'd rather pay someone I trust, and the rewards are good."

"Sounds interesting, but we'll need money to start up," said Patrick.

"That won't be a problem. The arrangement we have with the security company ends in April. If you take over, we'll pay you a year in advance.

Maybe some of the existing staff will come and work for you, that's if you think they're good enough.

There are many manufacturing companies in and around Boston, and they're all very secretive about their production methods. I have plenty of contacts there if you want to expand. Have a think about it."

"We will. It sounds like a good idea," I said.

"I've got some personal business to sort out

today so I'll see you all tomorrow. You'll be boarding at ten," said Ebenezer, limping away.

We spent the rest of the morning getting to know our travelling companions. James had a very dry sense of humour, and the conversation flowed with ease.

After some food at the hotel, we left them to their own devices and went for a walk around the city.

"I can't believe how overcrowded it is," I said.

"In a few years from now, they'll have trains on the streets, and it'll be even busier," replied my brother.

"Shall we walk down to the dock to see the Sirius?"

"I'd loved to," said Patrick.

We made our way there at a leisurely pace. Patrick's knowledge of the ship knew no bounds, and his enthusiasm was infectious. He began to tell me about it in great detail:

"The Sirius was built in Scotland in 1837. It became the first steamship to cross the Atlantic entirely on steam power. They had to burn the cabin furniture and a mast to get there. It was captained by a Cork man named Richard Roberts. It left Cork on the 04th April 1838, arriving in New York 18 days 4 hours and 22 minutes later."

When my brother acquired information about something, he could recall every minute detail, verbatim.

As we neared it, we saw a flotilla of vessels, all

shapes and sizes. The whole area was a hive of activity. Fishermen sat around in clusters, repairing nets and sorting through their catch of the day.

We saw the figurehead of the Sirius staring proudly at us. A dog, holding between its paws a star, representing the dog star Sirius it was named after.

My brother went into another of his spiels:

"It's a wooden-hulled side-wheel ship, 178 feet long, with two masts that stand either side of a central funnel.

It's got a two-cylinder steam engine that drives those two big paddle wheels on the side and can travel up to 12 knots.

When it left Cork in 1838, thousands of people lined the shores, cheering and shouting. She arrived in New York to an amazing fanfare. Thousands were there to greet her, even the mayor."

We watched them loading the cargo, then headed back to the city.

"Do you fancy going to the English Market?" I asked.

"Yes, I'd like to go to the new one too, St. Peter's."

We arrived at the heart of the commercial centre and stood outside the English Market, reluctant to enter. This was the affluent area of the city where the rich people lived, not an area we were accustomed to.

"Why are we hesitating? We're both dressed

like gentlemen," said Patrick.

"I don't know. Habit I suppose."

We passed stalls of every kind, targeting the wealthy classes of the city. Meat, fish, vegetables and exotic spices from the Far East were plentiful.

"This is unbelievable," said Patrick.

"If we had dressed in our old clothes, I don't think they would have let us in," I replied.

After a wander around, we headed for the Irish Market on Cornmarket Street. The differences between the two were obvious. The prices and food quality were far lower, aiming to serve the needs of the poor.

"It's a bit like Skibbereen Market," I said.

We felt uneasy as people stared at us in disdain. Our fine clothes looked totally out of place.

"I think we'd better head back while we still can," said Patrick.

"I agree, a good night's sleep will set us up well for tomorrow."

Before we went to bed that night, we pooled our money. With our wages and savings, we had 56 guineas, a small fortune.

Chapter 7

13th December 1841

At ten the following morning, we were standing at the wharf, waiting to board. I felt both nervous and excited, wondering what the future had in store for us.

"I'll see you in a few months," said Ebenezer.

"Hopefully, we'll have some answers for you by then," said Patrick.

A steady drizzle of rain fell as we crossed the rickety gangplank. It was slippery, so Teresa held on to James's arm to steady herself.

We were shown to a cabin with two berths and barely enough room to turn, but it satisfied our needs adequately.

Our trunks, which were very basic in construction, were stored under the bottom bunk.

The journey to Liverpool was uneventful. We were looked after courteously by the crew, and the table fare in the dining saloon was more than reasonable.

Patrick spent most of his time wandering the ship. He wanted to know how everything worked, and the crew were more than happy to answer his questions.

On the first morning, after breakfast, we stood on the deck with James and Teresa. We talked for hours despite the icy wind that blew from the north.

"How did you end up becoming a gambler, James?" asked Patrick.

"I suppose it was inevitable. I was born in New Orleans, the gambling capital of the world.

My grandparents emigrated from Cork around the turn of the century, but they both died from the Winter Fever. My mother was nineteen at the time and had to find a job to support herself. She worked as a dancer in a saloon, and that's where she met my father.

He was a professional poker player, and to him, it was like a religion. He played on the Mississippi riverboats and in the many gambling saloons in the city.

He taught me about its history: how the French sailors and traders brought a game to the city, called poque, which eventually evolved into poker.

He taught me how to read people and how to study their habits. He even taught me how to recognise a cheat when I saw one."

"What happened to him?"

"He was shot in an alleyway after winning a big pot of money. The perpetrator must have been watching him. It was a pretty lawless place back then and probably still is. My mother and I moved back to Cork five years ago."

"Has it been easy to give up?" I asked.

"Not at first, but it gets easier with time. I don't want to end up like my father.

Teresa made me promise that I'd never gamble with our money, and I intend to keep that promise.

It was the ultimatum I needed, and I don't want to lose her."

14th December 1841

The following day, we arrived in Liverpool: the largest provincial town in England and the second most important place after London.

We moored at the recently completed Coburg Dock. The same place the SS Britannia would leave from on the 03rd January.

A forest of masts stretched out before us, and a cacophony of noise filled our ears: the clatter of wheels from carters conveying their goods, bells ringing aboard ships, hydraulic cranes lifting heavy loads, heels clicking on cobbles, people yelling and shouting, and a newspaper crier in the distance selling the latest edition. I could see why it was the centre of trade, commerce and travel.

George Dutton, manager of the Cork Steamship Company in Liverpool, met the four of us at the end of the gangway. He shook our hands enthusiastically and handed me a piece of paper with directions to the hotel.

"The Adelphi is nearby, so I think it's best if you walk. It's in Ranelagh Place. One of our Carters will bring your luggage.

I'll be in touch in the next few days, but if there's anything you need in the meantime, let the manager of the hotel know."

We thanked him and headed for the hotel.

"It's nice to be back on solid ground again," said Teresa.

"Imagine what we'll feel like after our journey to America," said James.

"This place reminds me of Cork in some ways. Don't you think so, Sean?" asked Teresa.

"Yes, it does. That's because a lot of similar things have happened here. I read an article about it in the Cork Examiner a few months ago.

The wealthy merchants, who earned all their money from the blood, sweat and tears of others, used to live in this area, but they moved to the outskirts. Then the poor moved in. A similar thing happened in Cork.

In the last century, they made vast fortunes from the slave trade and from commodities like wool that they supplied to the textile mills in Manchester and Lancashire."

We walked along the cobbled road, passing unsavoury looking characters that stared at us with contempt.

The hustle and bustle of everyday life were present all around us, with horses and carts jostling for position on the overcrowded streets. The hardworking carters that drove them, were trying hard to keep the hotels, businesses and markets, supplied with food and raw materials.

Steeply terraced houses led away from the docks, full of poor families suffering from infectious diseases because of poor sanitation and overcrowding.

New arrivals aggravated the problem. They were everywhere, dragging their meagre belongings behind them.

"Why are there so many people here? There's not enough work for everyone, surely," said James.

"There are a lot of new projects about to start, like the Albert Docks, and the new hospital. That's why there's an influx of people," I replied.

Despite all this negativity, Liverpool was still a vibrant and exciting place to be. And we soon found out why.

At the corner of Brownlow Hill, we could hear the excited cries of a raucous crowd. Children's laughter and adult voices reverberated off the cobbles.

We turned the corner, and the reason became apparent. A flamboyant looking wagon, led by a team of eight cream coloured caparisoned horses, headed towards us.

"What's going on?" I asked a grinning young chimney sweep, whose teeth shone white against the black soot on his face.

"There's an American circus in town. They have a parade like this every day," he replied.

Dozen of horses and circus performers trailed behind the wagon, and comic tramps entertained the crowd with silliness.

The wagon passed us, and I could see the words, 'Richard Sands American Circus. Join us at our Splendid and Novel Pavilion,' emblazoned on the side.

"What's a novel Pavilion?" asked James.

"I've no idea, but there's only one way to find out. Shall we go?" I asked.

"Yes!" they all yelled.

None of us had ever been to a circus before, and this was an opportunity not to be missed.

"I'll speak to the manager of the Adelphi. Maybe he can get us tickets," I said.

A few minutes later, we met him. He was a very pleasant man with a genial personality.

"James Radley, at your service. I'm the manager of this fine establishment. I assume you're the party that's just arrived on the Sirius?"

"Yes, we are," I replied.

"I've been expecting you. Your rooms are ready, and lunch is being served. If there's anything you need during your stay, don't be afraid to ask."

"There is something you could do for us. We'd like four tickets for the circus, if you can manage it," I said.

"No problem. Would tomorrow's show be all right?"

"That would be perfect," I said.

The hotel had a warm homely atmosphere, not pretentious like some of the bigger establishments in the area. The facilities were good, and the location even better. Theatres, music halls and Lime Street Railway Station were only a stone's throw away.

We were shown to individual rooms that contained a bed big enough for a family.

Later that day, during our lunch, the manager presented us with four tickets and an itinerary for the show.

"That didn't take you long," I said.

"I went to see the owner, Mr Sands. He stayed here last year, and I got to know him well. There weren't many tickets left with tomorrow being a Saturday. It starts at one-thirty, so I'll make sure there's a carriage outside for you at one. I've added the price of the tickets to your account."

We all thanked him and continued eating.

After lunch, Patrick and I went exploring. James and Teresa stayed at the hotel.

"Where do you want to go?" I asked.

"I'd like to see the railway station in Lime Street. It's the first of its kind in the world, and it's only two minutes away. You can travel to Manchester from there."

"That's fine with me. Let's go," I said.

The station looked impressive and elegant with its four large gateways, two of which were nonfunctional. The hard-wearing platforms, made from Yorkstone, were packed with people getting ready to board the magnificent Lion steam engine.

There was work going on everywhere, and we had to be careful where we stepped. The station was being extended to cope with the increased volume of traffic it had experienced since its opening in 1836.

"This is the future. There'll be stations like this all over the world before long," said my brother.

The land across the road had been cleared in readiness for a new project. A sign had been placed in front of it with the legend: 'Saint George's Hall'.

"That's going to be big," said Patrick.

We continued along Lime Street and stopped for a drink at the Stork Hotel. It was on the north side of Queen Square.

As we neared, we could see a man stood at the entrance to the cellar doors. He was supervising a delivery of ale and had his back to the delivery cart.

The carter lost control of a keg, and it rolled towards the man. He just stood there, oblivious of the danger.

Patrick reacted first and pushed him out of the way.

"What the feck!" he yelled.

When he stood up, he realised how lucky he'd been.

"My God! I'd have gone headfirst into the cellar if you hadn't intervened."

"All's well that ends well. Is that a Dublin accent I hear?" asked Patrick.

"Yes, it is. Michael Murphy's the name or Mick if you prefer. I moved here from the Fair City ten years ago. This is my establishment, or it will be until Monday at least. I've just sold the place. This delivery is for the new owners. Why don't you come in and join me for a drink?"

"Thank you. That's where we were heading," said my brother. "My name's Patrick, and this is my brother, Sean. We're from Skibbereen."

"You're a long way from home. Are you here looking for work?"

"No, we're emigrating to Boston in America. We sail in January," I replied.

"It's a small world. My family and I are doing the same thing in March once I've tied up a few loose ends here. I've got a job lined up, managing a tavern. I hope to have my own place eventually, but I'd like to get to know the area first."

We entered a smoke-filled room packed with high-spirited folk and stood by the bar with Mick.

"Two pints of our finest for these two gentlemen, on the house!" yelled Mick.

"Yes, Dad! Two pints on their way!" yelled the barmaid.

"As you've probably guessed, that's my daughter, Rebecca."

"Pleased to meet you!" we both yelled.

Patrick never took his eyes off her from the moment we walked in. She was a beautiful looking woman with jet black hair that cascaded down to her waistline. Her skin was sallow and hinted at a Mediterranean ancestry.

"You're very busy, Mick. Is this normal?" I asked.

"It's always like this on a Friday, and it'll be even busier tomorrow, market day. A lot of our customers own fruit and veg shops in the area, but they've also got stall's in the market. In a few hours, the carters will start bringing supplies up from the warehouses at the harbour."

Rebecca placed our drinks in front of us and smiled politely at Patrick.

It was the first time I'd seen my brother lost for words. It didn't take a genius to see he was smitten.

"Do you have any plans for tomorrow evening?" asked Mick.

"Not really. We're going to the circus in the afternoon with some friends, but we're free in the evening," I replied.

"Why don't you call in for a drink with us? It's our last night before the new owners take over, and we've got some unfinished barrels to get rid of."

"That would be nice," said Patrick.

We finished our drinks, walked around the square, then headed back to the hotel for our evening meal.

Chapter 8

15ᵗʰ December 1841

The following afternoon, we all met up in the hotel's foyer. We were wrapped up warm, ready to face the bitterly cold wind that had picked up overnight.

I told them about the events at the Stork Hotel and that we'd make our own way back from the circus.

"Your carriage is outside. The circus is being held on the outskirts of town, on some waste ground," said James Ridley.

"What do you mean? It's normally held in a theatre," I said.

"You'll find out when you get there," replied James.

On the way, we passed stables galore, where hostlers were busy going about their daily duties. We passed a cooper's yard where the owner occupied himself making wooden casks, barrels, and buckets. Small business's existed on every street: a corset maker, a glover, a glasswright, a pork butcher, a basket maker and many more. They were all doing a roaring trade due to the volume of people on the streets.

Our driver dropped us a few hundred yards away to avoid the congestion, and the sight that beheld us was breathtaking.

"What the hell is that?" yelled James.

A giant canvas tent stood before us in all its majesty. We'd never seen anything like it.

"So, that's what they meant by a splendid and novel pavilion," said Patrick.

"It's a brilliant idea. They can travel all over the country with that and bring the circus to the masses," I said.

We produced our tickets and entered the most magnificent spacious Roman Amphitheatre. The interior decorations were also in the Roman style.

Thousand of people were sitting around a vast arena, waiting for the circus acts and horses to perform, and a full brass band blasted out popular tunes creating a euphoric atmosphere.

We were shown to our seats as the ringmaster introduced the comic tramps. They came on and performed humorous feats to warm up the crowd.

Richard Sands, a most versatile performer and owner of the circus, came on and performed a Roman riding act on four horses. It was breathtaking.

Levi North, their principal rider, performed tricks beyond belief, culminating in a somersault on a moving horse.

The most enthralling were the black-faced minstrels. They came on with their banjos and played electrifying music. Joel Walker Sweeney and Daniel Emmet played American songs that made my ears tingle.

High wire walkers performed amazing feats that kept everyone on the edge of their seat.

Acrobats ran down a wooden ramp onto a springboard, leaping into the air over animals and obstacles, but the most audacious act was kept until last and performed by Richard Sands.

It was called the Airwalk. Using rubber suction pads attached to his feet, he walked across a false ceiling high above the arena. The crowd were entranced and relieved when he made it to the other side. They showed their appreciation with rapturous applause.

"That was amazing," said Teresa.

"I've never seen minstrels perform before. It was strange and hypnotic, at the same time," I said.

"I loved the equestrian acts. I can't somersault on solid ground, let alone on horseback," said Patrick.

James and Teresa took the carriage back to the hotel whilst my brother and I walked to Queen Square.

We passed through a more affluent area of Liverpool, a far cry from the slums of the dock area. Well dressed families in the latest Paris fashions shopped in the more expensive emporiums. The women wore beautiful bonnets in pale blues and greens, and colourful scarves were the vogue, proving more popular than shawls.

Out of curiosity, we stopped at a confectioner's and stared at the cornucopia of sweets and delicacies on display in their window. Our mouths watered, but we resisted the temptation and moved on.

We arrived at the square as the sun was setting and the traders were packing down their stalls.

The Stork Hotel was packed to the rafters. News of the cheap ale had travelled fast, drawing in customers from all over Liverpool.

"Sean! Patrick! Over here! I've kept seats for you!" yelled Mick.

He was sitting in the corner with Rebecca, his wife and a very dark looking gentleman. We ordered drinks and joined them.

"This is my wife, Carolina. She's from Venice in Italy and moved here with her parents when she was a child. You've already met my daughter, and this is my very dear friend, Tom Olliver."

You could see where Mick's daughter had inherited her looks. Her mother had the same dark hair and sallow complexion.

Patrick sat next to Rebecca while I sat next to Mick.

"How was the circus?" asked Mick.

"Astounding. It was inside a giant canvas tent," I replied.

We explained the acts to them and described Richard Sands's Airwalk.

"It sounds thrilling. I'd like to go myself," said Tom.

His dark swarthy looks hinted at a Spanish or Gypsy ancestry, but his accent sounded well educated and coherent.

"Tom is a jockey. He's riding in the Grand Liverpool Steeplechase in March. He's going to win it this year, definitely," said Rebecca.

"I agree. He's riding a good horse, and he's got the experience to go with it," said Mick.

"Are you the favourite?" I asked.

"No, I'm not. A horse called Lottery is, but he's carrying a lot of extra weight because of a win at Cheltenham last year."

"What's the name of your horse?" asked Patrick.

He's called Gaylad. You should be able to get 8/1 at the moment, but the odds will probably shorten as we get closer to the time."

"What do you think, Sean? Shall we risk two shillings between us?"

"It's not until March. We won't be here to pick up the winnings," I replied.

"We'll be emigrating ourselves sometime after the race. If you win, we could bring the money to you. I'm sure we could arrange something," said Mick.

"You could leave your address at the Cork Steamship Company office. It's in the dock area. It would be nice to meet up, whether we win or lose," I said.

"No problem," said Mick.

We gave him the money and said a prayer for good fortune.

"Don't worry, Patrick. Your money will be safe with us, but if you win, I expect you to take me out for dinner in Boston," said Rebecca.

"I'd be honoured," said Patrick.

For the next few hours, the alcohol flowed, and it wasn't long before a singsong erupted.

Patrick and Rebecca were a match made in heaven and spent most of the evening in deep conversation.

Mick had to deal with a few inebriated men who were arguing, but he diffused the situation brilliantly and sent them on their way.

Two prostitutes walked in at one point, touting for business. Carolina gave them a look that would frighten the devil, and they soon moved on.

When our speech became undecipherable, we headed back to the hotel. Unbeknown to us, it had been raining, and the cobbles were perilous to walk on. We slipped a few times and had some strange looks off passers-by. We arrived in a dishevelled state and collapsed onto our beds in a drunken stupor.

The next few weeks passed quickly. We walked the streets of Liverpool until our muscles ached and saw most of the sights that were free to enter. James and Teresa accompanied us occasionally but kept to themselves for the majority of the time.

We went to the Botanical Garden a few times, only because it was free on Mondays and Fridays.

The Zoological Gardens on West Derby Road was an amazing experience. Antelope ran free through the grounds, and caged lions and tigers were on display. The main attraction was an elephant named Rajah, who would pick his keeper up with his trunk and place him back on the ground.

Patrick and Rebecca met up occasionally, and a romance was slowly blossoming.

Christmas Day at the hotel was like no other we'd experienced. We ate turkey, plum pudding and mince pies until we were too full to walk. The lobby and restaurant were festooned with mistletoe and holly, creating a Yuletide atmosphere and a children's choir sang carols in the foyer.

My brother and I loved every minute of it, but we would have given it all up for just one more Christmas with our family in Ireland.

02nd *January 1842*

One morning in January, I had the surprise of my life. We were discussing our future over breakfast when I noticed a small crowd gathering outside. I could see them through the restaurant window.

"What's going on out there?" asked Patrick, rhetorically.

"Let's go and find out," I replied.

We'd finished our breakfast, so we headed for the entrance, bumping into the hotel manager in the foyer.

"What's going on?" I asked.

"We have a celebrity and his wife staying with us for one night. They've stayed here before. Like yourselves, they're sailing to Boston tomorrow on the Britannia. Oh! here they are now!"

I looked up and couldn't believe my eyes. A young couple in their late twenties accompanied by a maid were walking towards us.

The gentleman was of average height and wore a brown frock coat, a flamboyant vest, and a fashionable scarf cravat that was fastened to the bosom in voluptuous folds.

"My God! It's Boz and his wife!" I yelled, excitedly.

"Do you know him?" asked the manager.

"Not exactly. We've been writing to each other for many years, but we've never actually met. I've seen his picture in the newspapers, frequently."

"Do you want me to introduce you?"

"Yes, please. He'll know my name when you mention it."

"Welcome to the Adelphi Hotel. It's so nice to see you again after such a long time. I have two young men here who'd like to meet you. They're travelling to Boston with you tomorrow. You know one of them by name but you've never met.

This is Patrick MacCarthy and his brother, Sean MacCarthy."

"My God! Sean MacCarthy from Skibbereen! I finally got round to reading your letter this morning. I was telling my wife about it earlier. This is my wife Catherine and her maid, Anne."

"Please to meet you. You should be so proud of yourselves. Your brave intervention in Skibbereen probably saved that man's life," said his wife.

"I think it probably saved ours too. It's giving us an amazing opportunity. I shall write to Father Sullivan and tell him about our meeting. He won't believe it," I said.

"Hopefully, we'll see more of each other on our journey. I don't like ships at the best of times so some pleasant conversation wouldn't go amiss," said Boz.

"I'll look forward to that immensely," I replied.

My brother and I returned to the restaurant and had our second coffee of the day.

"I can't believe it. Fancy meeting *Your Esteemed Friend*," said Patrick, laughing.

He'd called him that since we were young boys.

"It's a small world, Patrick."

Chapter 9

02ⁿᵈ *January 1842*

My brother spent his last evening in Liverpool with Rebecca. He wouldn't be seeing her until the end of March which was three months away.

I took advantage of my last night in the hotel by having a bath. I knew it would be my last for a while.

Feeling warm and relaxed, I sat at the small writing desk in my room and prepared to add the day's events into my journal. As I adjusted the gaslight above my head, there was a knock on the door. I opened it to find Boz standing there, holding an object wrapped in brown paper.

"This is for you, Sean. It's a birthday present. I know it's not until tomorrow, but I thought I'd give it to you now."

"How did you know?"

"You stated in your letter that you'd be travelling on your eighteenth birthday."

"Of course. How nice of you to remember."

"I'll be thirty myself in a month. How quick the time flies?"

"It does, indeed," I replied.

I removed the wrapping and discovered a book, signed on the title page:

To,
 Sean MacCarthy
  from

Your Esteemed Friend,
Boz.

It was familiar to me. I'd read the serialised version in Bentley's Miscellany.

"This is wonderful. I'll treasure it forever."

"Your welcome. I have to go now as we're having an early night. Our last sleep in a comfortable bed before we're confined to one of those claustrophobic cabins. I'll see you tomorrow and sleep well."

"I will, and thank you very much."

03rd *January 1842*

The following morning, I donned the travelling clothes I'd laid out the night before and went downstairs to join Patrick, James and Teresa for breakfast. They wished me a happy birthday, then I told them about Boz's gift.

"That was nice of him," said Patrick.

"Yes, it was. He's a very thoughtful man," I replied.

After breakfast, we said farewell to the staff and thanked them for their hospitality.

Our luggage had been taken to the ship the previous evening, so we walked to Coburg Dock where the Britannia was moored and ready for departure.

It looked magnificent in the distance with its two decks and side paddles. Three masts with full rigging stood proudly, and a bright red funnel glowed brightly against the skyline. The company that owned it was run by Samuel Cunard, a British Canadian shipping magnate.

George Dutton was waiting at the gangway with our tickets and an itinerary pertaining to our arrival in Boston.

Boz stood on the deck with his wife, waving to the tumultuous crowd that had gathered to see them off. He spoke to us as we passed.

"There are more people here than barnacles on the bottom of a ship," he said.

"That's the price of fame I'm afraid. I think they're here to see me," said Patrick, good humouredly.

"What's your accommodation like?" I asked.

"A bit incommodious to say the least. Nothing smaller for sleeping in has ever been made except for a coffin and trying to store our portmanteau of luggage is an impossibility. You're more likely to get a giraffe into a flowerpot."

My brother and I laughed at his inventiveness and headed below deck.

We met James and Teresa in the passageway.

"Our cabin's next to yours. It's small, but we'll manage. We're going on deck to wave to the crowd," said James.

"We'll follow you up," I replied.

Our home for the next few weeks was bigger than we thought and compared to our mud hut in Ireland, it was luxury. It was eight feet by six with two bunks and a settee. At the foot of the bottom berth stood a commode with two basins, two jugs and two chamber pots. A bottle of brandy for medicinal purposes rested on a shelf above the settee. Our luggage was stored neatly beneath the bottom bunk.

On our way to the deck, we passed a crew member who was busy removing the carpets, brocades and fine furnishings.

"Why are you doing that?" I asked.

"They're only there for show. When we hit bad weather, you'll understand," he replied.

On deck, I heard a strange noise coming from a storage room. I opened the door out of curiosity and found a cow staring at me in fright. The room was padded to protect the animal en route.

"At least we know where our milk is coming from," said Patrick.

As the ship cast off, the crowd of onlookers waved and cheered with zeal.

"Look! There's Rebecca!" I yelled.

Patrick's face lit up when he saw her. He blew kisses across the water until she disappeared from sight.

At five, a bell rang, summoning us for food. We crossed the deck and entered a dining saloon that looked more like a hearse with windows. Passengers were sitting on either side of a long table while stewards served hot and cold food. Above the table hung a rack that was fixed to the low roof. It was full of glasses and cruet stands.

Other stewards stood over a stove in the corner, warming their hands.

We sat with James and Teresa, and within minutes, food appeared: dishes full of steaming potatoes, a variety of meats, fresh fruit and ample amounts of alcohol.

We slept well that night with a little help from the brandy.

06th January 1842

A few days into our journey, things took a turn for the worse. During the night, a violent storm hit us, throwing me from my bunk onto the floor. The jug soon followed, landing squarely on my head. My brother helped me to my feet as a steady flow of seawater seeped under the door into our cabin. We were terrified and thought the ship was going down.

We went to investigate and came across James and his wife in the passageway, too scared to venture any further.

"I'm not going out there! We'll get washed overboard!" yelled James as the ship rolled from side to side.

I glanced on deck and could see the crew going about their business. The captain bellowed out orders through a speaking trumpet. Four crew members were battling with the ship's wheel, trying to keep us on course. Others attempted to get the sails down but were hampered by waves crashing around them.

The sea morphed into a mountain of angry water, turbulent and unforgiving, then morphed again into a deep valley. The rain poured from the sky in a continuous flow, mixing with the sea and burning our eyes. At one point, we held on for grim death as we rose into the air, only to come crashing down again with a force that rattled the ship from bow to stern. Sparks exploded from the funnel, and lightning lit up the sky in blinding flashes of white.

We returned to our cabin, sat on the settee and prayed for divine intervention.

"I'll be glad to put my feet back on solid ground," I said.

My brother was about to reply when he was overcome with nausea and threw up in the washbasin.

"You need a brandy and water," I said.

I poured some into a cup, added water and passed it to him. As I did so, the ship rolled from side to side, and by the time he received it, there was barely a mouthful left.

The storm persisted for several days. The ship rolled from side to side constantly, giving us an occasional glimpse of the horizon.

Boz and his wife spent most of their time in their cabin, suffering from seasickness.

Only a few of us ventured to the saloon. The rest stayed in their cabins.

The crew were in a bedraggled state, and you rarely saw one without a plaster or bandage on some part of his anatomy.

I ventured to the saloon on one occasion and found the captain in a very angry state.

"What's wrong?" I asked.

"My apologies, the food will be delayed for an hour. I found the chef drunk with an empty bottle of whisky in his hand. My men are putting the hose over him until he sobers up," he said.

"No problem, Captain. How's the ship looking?"

Some of the timbers protecting the paddles are damaged, but they're functioning. One of our life rafts got smashed to bits, but apart from that, she's fine. When we drop the mail off at Halifax, we'll do some repairs. You'll have about seven hours to explore the town before we sail on to Boston."

An hour later, my food arrived, which I devoured. My body was getting used to the constant rocking, but I longed for solid ground under my feet.

Not far from Halifax harbour, a heavy fog descended, causing us to strike a sandbank. We were stuck for hours and had to wait for the next tide to free us. Our captain handled the situation magnificently, and we were soon on our way.

Chapter 10

19th January 1842

On the morning of our arrival, we washed, dressed and made our way to the deck. The crew and officers were all lined up in crisp white uniforms. I looked up at the sun that shone brightly overhead.

"It's like a spring day in Ireland," I said.

"It certainly is if you ignore the cold wind," replied my brother.

We glided down a wide stream with land on either side, where white wooden houses stood amidst scatterings of snow. We could see wharves ahead with ships and crowded quays. The rambunctious noise of excited people lifted our spirits as we came alongside and made fast.

 We all jostled for position as a gangway was thrust out to meet us. We couldn't get off quick enough, and within minutes, we had disembarked.

"Terra firma at last," said Patrick.

"Thank God. I don't think I could have stuck another day," I replied.

"Do you mind if we join you?" asked James.

"By all means. We're going for a walk first, to get our land legs back, then we'll get some food somewhere. We have to be back on board in seven hours," I said.

"Sounds good to me," said James.

We could still feel the sway of the ship as we

walked like tipsy sailors towards the town.

A festive mood was present, and we soon found out why. Halifax had been incorporated as a city that day, and the inhabitants were in a celebratory mood. There were a few drunk people around, even at that early hour. The taverns and saloons were doing a roaring trade.

It was situated on the side of a hill, and at the top stood the Citadel, a great bastion of the British Empire where British soldiers were garrisoned. Several wide avenues ran down from it that were intersected with streets running parallel to the river.

The houses and buildings, apart from one or two, were made of wood, and each home had an elaborately decorated sleigh in the yard or nearby.

Gaslights were in the process of being fitted, and the city looked on the cusp of something special.

We walked towards Citadel Hill, then double backed towards the harbour.

"That tavern looks all right. Shall we try it?" asked Teresa, pointing.

"Why not? I'm starving," I replied.

We entered the Split Crow Tavern and found a vacant table by the window.

The place was full of character with oak beams, stained with the patina of time, spaced out evenly on the ceiling. Locals huddled around a huge open fireplace, warming their hands. A small group of men played cards boisterously while another group stood by the bar drinking whisky, celebrating the city's new status.

An elderly gentleman with a stooped back and long hair the colour of snow, approached us.

"Good day, what can I get you?" he inquired.

"Some of your local ale, please. Do you have a Bill of Fare?" I asked.

"Yes, but it's written in my head. We serve seafood mainly. Our scallops are delightful and by far our most popular dish. I can bring a selection of fish and vegetables for you to share if you like?"

We all nodded in agreement and watched him hobble away.

James was sitting with his back to the window, wearing a worried frown.

"What's wrong?" I asked.

"One of those gentlemen playing cards keeps staring at me oddly."

"Which one?" I asked.

"The one with the full beard and a head like a bull."

"Have you seen him before?"

"Not that I remember, but who knows? I've met a lot of gamblers over the years."

A few minutes later, our food arrived. A platter for four that included shrimps, haddock and salmon. Boiled potatoes and cabbage were served in a separate dish, along with homemade bread.

The smells were delightful, and my mouth salivated in anticipation.

"It's so nice to enjoy a meal with my feet firmly

on the ground," said Teresa.

"I agree, the food on the ship was nice but somewhat limited," I said.

At the end of our meal, James walked to the bar and ordered more ale. As he returned, the man with the bull's head stood up and blocked his way.

"I recognise you. We met in Dublin about five years ago. You cleaned me out in a poker game," he said, belligerently. "How about giving me a chance to win my money back?"

"I'm sorry, but I don't gamble anymore. Strict orders off my wife, I'm afraid," replied James.

"All I want is a chance to win my money back. Are you a man or a mouse?"

We all stood up, expecting trouble. Teresa got there first and placed herself between them.

"You heard what he said. He doesn't gamble anymore," she said, staring him in the face.

"Three shillings he won off me. I just want a chance to win it back. Perhaps he'll fight me for it."

James rolled up his sleeves in readiness.

"He's got no chance. The man's built like an ox," I whispered.

"I agree," said Patrick as he stood.

Bull's Head's friends also stood up, ready to join in the fray.

"If it's a fight you're looking for, I'll give you one," said Patrick.

"Nobody's fighting anyone! We'll resolve this like civilised people!" yelled Teresa. "Have you got two dollars you can afford to lose?"

"Of course I have," he replied.

"Then, I'll give you the chance to win your money back or are you afraid to gamble against a woman."

All his friends laughed and cajoled him along. Teresa took the money from her purse and laid it on the table.

"Put your money where your mouth is," she said.

He put his money on the table and looked at her with contempt.

"We'll cut the cards. The highest number takes all," she said.

Bull's head went first. A small bead of sweat trickled down his brow as he reached out his hand. He knew that if he lost against a woman, he'd be a laughingstock. He cut the cards, producing the six of hearts.

"A middle card. Could be worse, I suppose," said Teresa.

She put her hand out slowly, cut the cards, and turned over the six of spades.

"A draw game!" she yelled. "At least you've broken even."

Bull's Head looked at her in relief. At least his reputation remained intact. His friends laughed, and before long they were all laughing.

They returned to their tables, both parties content with the outcome.

"You're a crazy woman. I thought you didn't like gambling," said James.

"I don't like you gambling. There's a big difference."

"You defused the situation brilliantly, Teresa. It would have been a bloodbath otherwise," I said.

"Yes, you're right, but I think we'd better head back to the ship. They're getting drunker by the minute, and we don't want any more trouble."

"That's a perfect example of my past catching up with me. I've met some dodgy characters over the years," said James as we exited the tavern.

"Did you ever cross paths with a man named Charles Smithers? Our parents are tenants on his grandfather's land," I said.

"I've never met him personally, but his reputation precedes him. He's known as a cheat and uses every trick in the book. He normally plays against inexperienced players, not professionals like myself."

We finished our drinks and headed back. We thought of going into one of the many saloons near the harbour, but they were men only and packed to the rafters.

Captain Hewitt was standing at the end of the gangway when we boarded.

"You're early," he said.

I explained the events at the tavern, and how Teresa had saved the day.

"That was quick thinking. Someone got stabbed there not so long ago. You had a lucky escape."

"How long before we sail?" I asked.

"About an hour. We need to go before the frost comes in. The harbour tends to freeze over this time of year."

The rest of them went to their cabins while I stayed on deck with the captain.

"Do you know much about Boston?" he asked.

"Only what I've read. I know that Captain John Smith explored the coastline in 1614 and named the area New England to make it sound more attractive to settlers."

"That's right, Sean, but when the Europeans arrived, they brought smallpox with them. They wiped out more than half of the indigenous people."

"I read about that somewhere. The Puritans from England founded the city in 1630. They named it after the town in Lincolnshire."

"They were a tough lot those Puritans and not very tolerant of other religions. It's still the same today. Most of the inhabitants are Protestant. Did you know that many of the key events of the Revolutionary war took place in or near Boston?" asked the captain.

"Yes, I did. The Boston Massacre and the Boston Tea Party of course."

"That's right. The massacre took place outside the Boston Custom House. A mob of patriots started throwing snowballs at a soldier who was standing guard outside. It escalated from there and ending up with five people getting killed.

My grandfather was a member of an

organisation called the Sons of Liberty. They were furious at being taxed with no representation in parliament. He took part in the Boston Tea Party though he never admitted it outright.

It happened at Griffin Wharf. The colonists dressed up as Native Americans and threw forty five tons of tea into the harbour. It took them nearly three hours."

"What's Boston like as a city?" I asked.

"I think you'll love it. It's the most civilised city in America. It's got six daily newspapers, a world renowned university and two professional theatres: the Tremont and the National.

Quincy Market is well worth a visit. Their produce is as fresh as it gets. I remember them building it when I was a child. They named it after the mayor, Josiah Quincy. Do you like oysters?"

"I've never tried them," I replied.

"Go to the Atwood and Bacon Oyster House on Union Street. The oysters there are exquisite, and the clam chowder is to die for."

"Thank you, It sounds delightful."

"You're a good friend of Boz's, aren't you?" asked the captain.

"Yes, I've known him for a long time. We've been writing to each other for many years. We stayed in the same hotel in Liverpool, but that was the first time I'd met him in person."

"He's very popular in America. There'll be a lot of press there when we arrive and maybe even the mayor."

"I didn't know his fame stretched that far," I said.

"He wants to set up an international copyright law in America because he doesn't get paid any royalties. Many people are getting rich on the back of his name."

"That doesn't seem fair," I said.

"It's not, but trying to implement change is difficult."

Over the next hour, the passengers returned, and we were soon on our way.

We hit foul weather at the Bay of Fundy but apart from that, the rest of the journey was good.

Chapter 11

22ⁿᵈ January 1842

After eighteen horrendous days at sea, we docked at Boston's Long Wharf.

I could see where it got its name from. It extended one-third of a mile from the shoreline, into deep water, allowing the bigger ships to moor.

It was a bitterly cold evening, and a blanket of snow covered the ground. We wrapped up warm in our coats, gloves and scarves, and went up on deck. James and Teresa were already there, eager to disembark.

"According to the itinerary, we need to meet someone called Phineas," said James.

"I know, but I think we'd better wait until the crowd dissipates," I said.

Captain Hewitt had been right. A large cheering assemblage had gathered on the wharf to greet Boz. As soon as the gangway came to rest, chaos ensued. Journalists and editors leapt on board, eager to get an interview.

With great difficulty, Boz and his entourage were led to a carriage. I watched them disappear into the distance and wondered if I'd ever see them again.

Phineas was waiting at the end of the gangway, dressed in a grey fur coat with the collar turned up.

I guessed his age at around thirty. He was six

feet tall but gave the impression of being taller because of his top hat. He smiled, and his piercing blue eyes lit up like sapphires.

"You must be Phineas Finn," I said.

"At your service," he replied, bowing politely. "I have a carriage waiting, and your luggage will follow shortly. You'll be staying at a boarding house owned by the Cork Steamship Company. It's a beautiful place on Hawkins Street, in the heart of the city. All your meals and laundry are included, so you've nothing to worry about."

My brother and I were delighted. It meant that we could save most of what we earned.

"I assume you know why we're here?" asked Patrick.

"Yes, Ebenezer explained everything in his letter. We'll be offloading the cargo in the morning at nine if you want to come down and oversee. I'll meet you in my office which is on the right here, next to our warehouse," he said, pointing.

"That's pretty close to the ship," replied Patrick.

"Yes, it is. It won't take long to unload."

We waddled like ducks across the snow, holding on to each other for support and with the help of the coachman, we boarded safely.

The wheels of our carriage struggled to gain purchase on the frozen ground as we set off down State Street. A flurry of snow fell, illuminated by the orange glow of the gaslights. Crowds of people ambled along the wide snowy streets, wrapped up in warm winter clothes. Even the lower classes were well turned out compared to the poor of Liverpool and Cork.

The buildings were magnificent with their decorative facades and Greek pillars, built to withstand the ravages of time. Shop board signs glowed with fresh paint, and gilded letters shone in the moonlight. Even the doorknobs gleamed radiantly.

"That's a fine looking building over there. It looks new," I said, pointing.

"It's the Merchant Exchange and the focal point for business in the city. It opened recently. It's well worth a visit.

The red brick building on the left with the fancy balcony is the Old State House. It's one of the oldest buildings in Boston, and a fine example of Georgian architecture. It was Boston City Hall until recently, but it's been converted for commercial use. There's an excellent tailor's in there that I use.

The street going off to the left is Washington Street. There are some fine buildings along there too," said Phineas.

"How many are staying at the boarding-house?" asked James.

"Just you four for now, so there'll be plenty of room. It's run by a lady named Mary Proudfoot and her fourteen year old daughter. Her husband used to work for us, but he died in a tragic accident about four years ago whilst unloading cargo at the wharf."

"That's so sad," said Teresa.

"Mary and I have been courting each other for the last few months. She's an amazing woman," said Phineas.

"Where does Ebenezer stay when he's here?" asked Patrick.

"He owns a property on Beacon Hill, opposite the common."

"What about you? Do you live close by?" I asked.

"Yes, I do. I own a property in Merrimack Street, just around the corner. My parents passed away a few years ago, and I used my inheritance to buy it. They owned a farm near Concord that my brother now owns, but farming isn't the life for me. I prefer the city."

A few minutes later, we arrived at our new home which was directly opposite the public school. Mary and her daughter were waiting outside to greet us.

Mary had the look of a woman used to hard work. She was in her late thirties with long auburn hair tied up in a bun.

"Welcome to Boston," she said.

We all shook hands and introduced ourselves.

"I've prepared hot baths for you. After such a long journey, I thought you'd be glad of it."

"That's perfect. I can't wait to change into clean clothes," said Teresa.

"Here are your keys. There's one for the main entrance and one for your rooms. I'd go up now if I were you while the water's still hot. When your luggage arrives, I'll send it straight up.

Dinner will be served at 7.30 and your breakfast in the morning will be between 7 and 8. There's a map of the city in your rooms to help you get your bearings."

We thanked her for her foresight. A hot bath was something we'd been dreaming of for weeks.

Phineas handed James a piece of paper.

"That's the address of Ebenezer's Drapery and Menswear. It's opposite the Boston Theatre on Federal Street. It's only a short walk from here. Everyone knows where it is, so if you get lost, just ask someone."

"That's fine. I'm sure we'll find it."

"Well, I'll be on my way. I'll see you two in the morning at the Long Wharf," said Phineas.

We all waved him off, then followed Mary into the property.

Our accommodation exceeded our expectations. The living area had two comfortable armchairs, a small Chippendale table, two dining chairs and a kneehole writing desk next to the window. Brightly coloured rugs in reds and blues covered the stone flag floor, and an Adams fireplace emitted heat into the room. It was finished off with drapery that matched the rugs perfectly.

Two bedrooms led off from the living area, each with a commode. A hot bath stood by the fire, and two towels lay on the floor in front of it.

"This is amazing, Mary. Thank you for

everything," I said.

"Your welcome, and I'll see you later for dinner."

Patrick was in the bath singing to himself when the luggage arrived. Two carters brought them up and placed them at the foot of our beds.

"These trunks are wet. When they dry, the wood will twist and warp. I think you'll need some new ones," said one of them.

"We'll have to buy something sturdier next time, although, I don't see us going anywhere soon," I replied.

After dinner that evening, we went for a short walk around the nearby streets. We came upon the Atwood and Bacon Oyster House on Union Street.

"Captain Hewitt recommended this place. He said the oysters are exquisite," I said.

"We'll have to try it one day. It'll be another first for us," replied my brother.

We retired early that night feeling fatigued and slept soundly.

Chapter 12

23rd January 1842

We woke at seven to the sound of church bells. By eight, we were sitting at the dining table downstairs.

Patrick was studying the map of the city when Mary's daughter walked in.

"Good morning! How are you today?"

"Very well, thank you," we both replied.

"What's your name?" I asked.

"Claire, and I'm in a jovial mood today. I've just received confirmation from the Lowell Textile Mills. I can start work there in two weeks."

"That's good news. Is it a nice place to work?" asked Patrick.

"It's hard work for low pay, but the conditions are good. Single girls have to stay at a boarding house near the mill. There are strict rules though. I have to be in my room by ten and attend church regularly. After paying my rent, I'll still have money over to pay for night school."

"That sounds good. How far away is Lowell?" asked Patrick.

"It's just under an hour. You can get there on the Boston to Lowell Railroad."

"Do you think your mother will manage without you?" I asked.

"That's what worries me. She says she will, but I'm not so sure."

James and Teresa joined us as our breakfast arrived: beans and warm homemade bread.

"That smells nice," said James.

"It certainly does, and I'm famished," I replied.

After breakfast, we began our walk to the waterside.

We passed the Mayhew School and could hear the high pitched voices of excited pupils throwing snowballs at each other.

"There's nothing angelic about that sound," I said.

The snow was thawing, revealing clumps of horse deposit, pulverised into the cobbles. It was treacherous to walk on, but we arrived safely and in one piece.

The warehouse was in a state of preparedness, and a haggard looking man who we assumed was security stood outside. He wore a black suit and a flat cap that had seen better days.

Phineas was standing outside with a cup of something warm in his hand. Tendrils of vapour rose from it, mixing with the frosty morning air.

"Good morning, gentlemen. They're just about to unload the cargo. Come into my office, and we'll go through the paperwork," he said.

The office was warm and cosy. Hot coals burned brightly in a small cast iron fireplace. A carved walnut table with four matching high-back chairs took up the bulk of the room, and matching storage cabinets lined the walls.

We sat around the table, and Phineas explained

the process.

"You don't have to worry about the unloading of the cargo. I check everything as it arrives, and it always tallies up as it should. The problem is somewhere between the warehouse and the customer.

We have a variety of things arriving today: lard, honey, butter, salted beef and a large quantity of Guinness, 50 barrels to be exact."

"I didn't think Guinness could travel. I thought it would go off," I said.

"No, It's a special brew for export. Extra hops and alcohol help to preserve it. They've been making it for a long time. Some people call it West Indian Porter because it's exported there for the Irish working in the Caribbean."

"How many people work on security at night?" asked Patrick, changing the subject.

"Just one."

"What about during the day?"

"The same, but the carters are always back and fore picking up goods for delivery."

"If I was going to steal anything, I'd do it at night. Do security know who we are and what we're doing here?" asked Patrick.

"No, we haven't told anyone. Would you like to look around the warehouse?"

"Yes, I've got an idea and I want to see if it's feasible," said Patrick.

We entered the warehouse and took in our surroundings. The stock was stored in individual blocks, three yards square by three yards high. Butter and lard were stored at the back and salted beef in the middle. Miscellaneous products were on the opposite side in a more haphazard fashion. Barrels of Guinness were stacked near the entrance, for easy access.

A small glass-fronted office stood opposite the butter where the night watchman could sit in relative comfort.

"Does the butter go there?" asked Patrick, pointing to a space opposite the office.

"Yes, It's on its way."

"Could you have them stacked as normal but with a space in the middle, enough for two people to squeeze into?" asked Patrick.

"Yes, we can do that," replied Phineas.

I could see my brother's plan straight away. We could hide in there and surprise any unwelcome visitors.

"Leave a tiny opening on either side so we can see out," said Patrick.

"No problem. Leave it with me."

"How are we going to get into the hiding place without being seen?" I asked.

"That's easy," said Phineas. "The day shift finishes at 7:30 pm, and the night shift starts at 08:00 pm. That leaves a thirty minute window for you to sneak in. I'm always here for the shift changeover. I can make sure there's food, water and blankets there for you. It'll get cold at night."

"That would be perfect. We'll start tomorrow

evening and meet you here at 07.40. What do you think, Sean?" asked my brother.

"Sounds good to me. A good night's sleep tonight will put us in good stead. What about local law and order? Do they patrol at night?" I asked.

"The Boston Watch do. You'll know them when you see them. They carry a badge of office, a rattle and a six-foot pole painted blue and white. The pole's got a hook on one end and a bill on the other. They use the hook to grab fleeing criminals and the bill as a weapon. The rattle's used to call for help.

There's also a handful of police officers controlled by the city marshal, but they only work during the day."

"I think that's everything, Phineas. We'll see you tomorrow evening," I said.

"Okay. What are your plans for the rest of the day?"

"We're going to familiarise ourselves with the city and maybe try some oysters," replied Patrick.

"You won't be disappointed."

We found Quincy Market and Faneuil Hall on the map and headed there. It wasn't far, just a short walk from the waterside.

The new market was a beautiful granite indoor pavilion, over five hundred feet long and built in the Greek revival style. Four Doric columns stood at the main entrance, which led to a long hallway filled with a burgeoning array of stalls. The interior was mainly red brick with cast-iron columns.

We walked down the hallway until we came to a spacious area with an ornate domed ceiling. People were sitting around sipping hot drinks and chatting.

"This place is impressive," said Patrick.

"I read about it recently. It used to be just Faneuil Hall, and the North and South Markets, then they built this about twenty years ago. The mayor, Josiah Quincy, was working in his office above the hall, staring out of the window. He realised that the current market was no longer sufficient to cater for the needs of the city, so he decided to build a new one.

Faneuil Hall is steeped with history. It's where Samuel Adams spoke to the people of Boston regarding independence and where George Washington toasted the nation on its first birthday. It's all in the books that Kath lent me."

"Have you been thinking about her?" asked Patrick.

"I have, but it's like you said: Rich Protestants don't mix with poor Catholics."

"We're not poor by far, and we could end up being wealthy if we build up the security business. Would you consider converting to Protestantism?" asked Patrick.

"I would, but I don't think Ma would be too happy about it, or Father Sullivan. Da wouldn't be bothered one way or the other. Would you convert?"

"Without hesitation. There are not many

opportunities for Catholics here or in Ireland. It would certainly help our business."

"We should look into it. Maybe Ebeneezer could point us in the right direction," I said.

We continued past the market, turned right onto Union Street and arrived at the Atwood and Bacon Oyster House.

We sat on stools at the semi-circular bar, and a barman with short black hair and an ebullient personality took our order: Guinness and a half dozen stewed oysters each.

A few minutes later they arrived, and the waiter shucked them in front of us.

Patrick started laughing and said, "Do you remember when Da spoke to us about emigrating? He said the worlds our oyster. I didn't think we'd end up eating them."

"I wish they could see us now. We'll have to write to them tonight. They'll be eager to hear from us," I said.

"Yes, we'll do it later. I've been thinking about keeping a journal like you. I want something to pass on to my children, that's if I have any."

"Good idea, Patrick."

My taste buds tingled in anticipation. I picked up my first oyster, placed it on my tongue and closed my eyes. The flavours bounced around my mouth in a frenzy.

"It taste's like the sea," I said.

"I know what you mean. It's hard to explain, but you're right. Do you want some more?"

"Why not?"

"The same again please, Barman," yelled Patrick.

"Certainly Sir, and where do you gentlemen hail from? Do I hear an Irish accent?"

"Yes, you do. We're from Skibbereen, outside Cork," replied Patrick.

"And is this your first time to try oysters?"

"Yes, it is. They're delightful," I replied.

"Well, you certainly came to the right place. There's a lot of history attached to this building. Did you know that the present King of France, Louis Philippe, used to be one of our regulars? When he was in exile, he lived upstairs and earned his living teaching French to the fashionable young ladies of Boston."

"That's interesting. The captain of the ship we arrived on recommended you," I said.

"Would that be Captain Hewitt?"

"Yes, he said your oysters were the best," I said.

"How nice of him. He was in here yesterday, actually."

After lunch, we explored the city and ended up in Beacon Hill, the affluent area of Boston. The brick row houses were grandiose and reserved for the wealthier classes. The New State House was nearby and built in the Greek Revival style. It looked spectacular with its light yellow dome.

We arrived back at Hawkins Street in the early evening and wrote a letter to our parents. We informed them of our trials and tribulations during the journey, and Patrick told them about Rebecca and her family.

Chapter 13

24th January 1842

The following evening, we arrived at the warehouse at 07.40. Freezing fog drifted inland from the sea, creating an eerie atmosphere.

Phineas was waiting outside, rubbing his arms against his body to stay warm. I handed him the letter that my brother and I had wrote for our parents.

"Could you make sure this gets on the next steamer back to Cork?"

"No problem. Leave it with me," he replied. "I've prepared your hideout and left some water and bread for you. There are two blankets in there to keep you warm, which you're going to need if the temperature keeps dropping."

Phineas handed me a letter of his own and said, "Bill is the name of the watchman on duty tonight. If anything happens or you get discovered, give him this. It explains everything. I'll be here by seven in the morning before the day shift starts."

We both nodded and made our way inside. We squeezed into the block and made ourselves comfortable. There were a few tiny gaps in each wall, big enough to see through but not too big as to reveal our presence.

"It's going to be a long night," I said.

"I'm glad we put extra layers on. I'm colder than a polar bear's balls," said Patrick, laughing.

A few minutes later, we heard Phineas's voice. The night watchman had arrived.

I squinted through the gap and saw Bill standing in the doorway. His silhouette cast a shadow against the moonlight.

He entered, enabling me to see him more clearly. He was a slovenly looking man in his early forties with a drinkers paunch. A black bag hung from his shoulder, and the sound of glass against glass reverberated from within.

He entered the office and sat in the comfortable leather chair with his feet resting on the desk.

The main door to the warehouse was unlocked which I thought was strange. A level of complacency has set in that I was not happy about.

25th January 1842

Patrick and I took turns watching, and at close to midnight, I heard a clinking sound. Bill produced a bottle of whisky and a glass from his bag, then poured himself a stiff measure.

He carried on that way for the next two hours, eventually passing out.

Patrick and I looked at each other in disbelief.

"How long has been getting away with this?" I whispered.

"Who knows?" replied my brother.

A few minutes later, we heard a noise. It was the warehouse door creaking on its hinges.

Two very short people dressed in black crept in

confidently. They both wore masks to hide their identity. Neither of them spoke to each other. They just went about their business in a very cocksure manner.

One of them went back outside and wheeled in a handcart. It was just the right size to fit through the doorway.

The other one rolled a barrel of Guinness towards it. With one each end, they lifted the barrel onto the cart.

That's when my brother and I made our move. Patrick ran to the door to block their exit while I attacked the nearest one to me.

I dragged him to the floor and held him there with my knees. He never moved. He just yelled at me in a high pitched voice.

"Please don't hurt me!"

I pulled the mask off, and my suspicions were confirmed. It was a young girl, about twelve years of age.

The other one tore off his mask and yelled at me, "Get off my sister!"

He was even younger than the girl, about ten years of age. They both had long blond hair in desperate need of a wash.

"What are you doing stealing at your age? You could end up on the gallows for this," said Patrick.

"It's steal or starve," said the girl.

We took them into the office where Bill was still fast asleep. I shook him vigorously, and eventually, he woke up.

"What the hell's going on?" he slurred.

"This letter off Phineas explains everything. Now piss off home and don't come back," said Patrick, angrily.

Bill rose from his chair, picked up his bag, and staggered towards the door.

"Sit down. I want to ask you some questions, and I want the truth. What are your names?" I asked.

"My name is Sarah Brown, and my brother is Oliver, like Oliver Twist."

Her brother looked at me sheepishly.

"Where are your parents?"

"Our house burned down a year ago, and they were both killed. We got out, and we've been living on the streets ever since. I think people assumed we were dead as nobody came looking for us.

We'd rather live like this than be separated. They'd put me in the female asylum, and God knows where my brother would end up."

"Where do you live now?" I asked.

"There's a small stable attached to the Warren Tavern in Charlestown. The owner, Charles Smithers, lets us stay there as long we produce the odd barrel of Guinness and some blocks of butter.

He's a horrible man. He threatened to report us if we didn't carry on stealing for him."

"He's calling your bluff. If he reported you, he'd end up in trouble himself," said Patrick.

"How long have you been stealing from us?" I asked.

"Since our parents died. We saw the night watchman staggering to work drunk one night. We knew he wouldn't be able to stay awake in that state.

When we found the door unlocked, we couldn't believe it. We took some butter to sell the first time, and it escalated from there."

I looked at them both with incredulity. How they'd survived so long was a miracle.

"From now on, you can stay in the office next door. You'll be safe there until we find something more suitable. We'll make sure you stay together no matter what happens," I said.

Patrick gave them our food and water, then we went outside to talk.

"Charles Smithers! It's funny how his name keeps popping up. It's time someone taught him a lesson," I said.

"What are we going to do with them?" asked Patrick.

"I'm not sure. They deserve a better start in life after what's happened to them."

"I've got an idea," said Patrick. "Why don't we speak to Mary? If her daughter Claire is going to work in the mill, maybe Mary will take them in. They could help out around the place and earn their keep."

"That's a good idea. When Phineas arrives, we'll speak to him about it."

Phineas arrived at seven. He couldn't believe his eyes when he saw the two children.

I went over their story, and he listened sympathetically.

"I'm not surprised Charles Smithers is involved. He's got his fingers in all sorts of shady deals. I've been to the Warren Tavern a few times. He lures sailors into the place with the offer of free drinks, then fleeces them over a game of poker. He's the lowest of the low. I heard he's gone back to Ireland on business," he said.

"We know of his reputation. His grandfather is the same type and totally devoid of empathy. He owns the land our parents live on in Skibbereen," said Patrick.

"We can't leave them on the street. What are we going to do with them?" asked Phineas.

I explained our intentions, and he agreed with us.

"I think Mary will be glad of the help. I don't mind chipping in financially if necessary," he said.

"Will you keep an eye on them today? Patrick and I will have a chat with Mary. We have to go to the Boston bank as well," I said.

"Not a problem. They can come with me. I have to speak to the security company later because we need someone to work tonight."

"We're going to take over the security in April. We've already spoken to Ebenezer about it. In fact, it was his idea," said Patrick.

"I think you'll do very well, and with Ebenezer's contacts, you could expand. You should mention it to the bank manager while you're there.

His name's Francis Brown, and he's a good friend of Ebenezer's."

"We'll do that, and thanks, Phineas. We'll call back this evening. Hopefully, we'll have some good news," I said.

Patrick and I went back inside and spoke to Sarah and Oliver.

"Stay with Phineas for the day while we sort something out for you. We'll be back later," I said.

As we were leaving, Sarah began to sob.

"What's wrong?" asked Patrick.

"I don't know. We've been living in fear for a long time, and acts of kindness are not something we're used to."

"You'll be safe from now on. I promise you," said Patrick.

We arrived back at Hawkins Street in time for breakfast.

James and Teresa were sitting at the dining table, eating. We told them what had happened and they couldn't believe it.

"How are things at the drapery?" asked Patrick.

"We're getting there. It needed a bit of organising, and James is getting the books in order," replied Teresa.

Claire walked in carrying two plates of bacon, beans and eggs.

"Good morning. Would you like the same?"

"Yes, please," we replied.

"Would you ask your mother to join us when

she's finished her chores? There's something we'd like to discuss with her," I said.

"I'll let her know," she replied, scurrying off to the kitchen.

James and Teresa left for work, leaving us alone in the dining room. After breakfast, Mary joined us with a pot of coffee and three cups.

"I've left Claire to do the cleaning up. She's a great help around the house, and I'm going to miss her when she's gone," she said.

"She told us about it. It's the reason we wanted to talk to you," I said.

"What do you mean?"

"A situation occurred last night that's left us in a dilemma," I said and went on to explain.

Mary looked at us with one eyebrow raised.

"How do I come into it?" she asked.

"We were wondering if you'd take them in. They could earn their keep by helping around the house. They're not bad children. They just need the chance of a normal life," I said.

"Phineas has offered to help financially if necessary," said Patrick.

"How old are they?" asked Mary.

"Sarah is twelve, and her brother's ten," I replied.

"Let me think on it for a few hours. It's a big responsibility to take on," she said.

"Certainly, we'll speak to you later."

Chapter 14

We arrived at the bank as the doors were opening to a brand new day. We mentioned Ebenezer's name to the teller, and within minutes we were in the manager's office.

He was sitting behind his desk, looking us up and down as if appraising our wealth. He was a strange looking character with a non-existent chin, giving him the appearance of a tortoise.

"Good morning, Mr Brown. I'm Sean MacCarthy, and this is my brother Patrick. I believe Ebenezer Foley has opened accounts for us," I said.

"Yes, he has. I've been expecting you. I have some papers here for you to sign."

His desk was immaculate. An ornate brass ink well stood at the front, along with a matching dip pen. The rest of it was clear of clutter apart from a small stack of documents to his right.

He took two documents from the stack and placed them on the table in front of us.

"You need to sign these. I believe you work in security. Is that right?" he asked.

"Yes, we do. We're starting up our own company. Ebenezer has offered us the contract when it comes up for renewal in April. We'll be looking to expand in the future so any advice would be much appreciated," said Patrick.

"I suggest you get some calling cards made. You never know who you're going to bump into when you're out and about. Most of the Boston elite live in and around Beacon Hill. These are the people who own businesses in Boston, ex Harvard types if you know what I mean. The majority of them are the descendants of the original colonists that came over on the Mayflower. They're very fastidious as to who they let into their circle, especially if you're from some other denomination other than Protestant. It took Ebenezer a long time to be accepted.

Things are changing rapidly, though. New industries are opening up on the outskirts of Boston every day. They're a new breed of businessmen with some very innovative ideas. For example, I spoke to someone yesterday who's invented a machine to make nuts and bolts. These people are very secretive about their inventions, and I'm sure they'd be happy to do business with you. Have you got a name for your company?"

"Safe and Sound Security," I replied.

"Three S's. That sounds good. You'll need a business account under the company name. I'll sort that out for you."

We thanked him, then headed home for some much needed sleep.

We woke at 5:30 pm feeling refreshed and went downstairs to see if Mary had come to a decision.

Claire brought us coffee, and we sat at the dining table to discuss it.

"I'm not averse to the idea, but I'd like to meet them first. Phineas and I are having dinner here this evening at eight. Perhaps you can bring them along, and they can eat with us. If I'm happy with what I see, they can stay. There's a room downstairs with two beds they can use.

I could certainly do with the help when Claire leaves, but I won't take any nonsense. If they misbehave in any way or bring trouble to my door, they'll be out on the street."

"We understand totally. We'll make sure they're here by eight, in time for dinner," said Patrick.

"I want them here earlier than that, by seven if possible. They'll need a bath and some clean clothes. Claire's old clothes will fit Sarah, and I'll sort something out for the boy."

We walked down to the warehouse and found Phineas supervising the children.

The same scruffy security guard we'd seen the day before stood outside, looking us up and down with a wary eye.

"We'll have to get some sort of uniform sorted out when we take over. We can't have people standing around looking like vagabonds," said Patrick.

"I agree. Presentation is everything," I replied.

Sarah was loading a cart with butter while her brother busied himself sweeping the floor.

They both looked far happier than they did the night before, Sarah in particular. The burden of responsibility had been lifted off her shoulders, and she looked more like a twelve year old.

We all sat in the office while I explained the

situation. The children were delighted and looked forward to a bath and some clean clothes.

"Best of behaviour, and don't forget your manners. Any nonsense and Mary will cast you onto the street," said Patrick.

They both nodded in agreement, then continued with their work.

"How have they been, Phineas?" I asked.

"Fine. I took them for something to eat at the Green Dragon Tavern in Union Street. They'd been there before with their father. They know more about the history of the place than me."

"We passed it the other day. What history?" I asked.

"It was the local watering hole of the Sons of Liberty. Some of their best plots against the Redcoats were hatched there, including the Boston Tea Party."

"Perhaps we can pop in there one day," said Patrick.

Phineas had arranged for the night watchman to come in early. As soon as he arrived, we headed back home for dinner.

Mary fussed over the children like a mother hen. She showed them to their room, where a bath had been prepared. They were soon squeaky clean and dressed in their new clothes.

My brother and I joined James and Teresa in the dining room. We were just finishing our dinner when Sarah and Oliver walked in looking unrecognisable. Months of ingrained dirt had been scrubbed from their bodies, and their skin glowed.

Sarah's hair had been put up in a bun, and Oliver looked like a different child in his brand new clothes.

"My God! What a transformation! You look almost human!" yelled Patrick.

James and Teresa joined us for a walk, so we could leave them in peace to enjoy their dinner.

26th January 1842

The following morning, Mary served us breakfast, grinning from ear to ear.

"What are you looking so happy about? Did the children behave last night?" I asked.

"Yes, they did. Their behaviour was exempary. They're well educated and well mannered although, Oliver needs some work on his reading.

Once we've gone through the proper procedures regarding adoption, we'll enrol them at the Mayhew school across the road, or the Mayhem as I call it."

"You just said we," I said.

"That's why I'm so happy this morning. Last night, after the children had gone to bed, Phineas proposed to me, and I said yes."

We both stood up and gave her a big hug.

"Congratulations! We haven't known Phineas for long, but he seems like a very caring person. I'm sure you'll be happy together," I said.

Chapter 15

The next few weeks flew by. Julie started her job at the mill, and the children took over her chores with ease.

We got to know the security guards and promised jobs to the ones we thought were suitable. They recommended friends who were reliable and before long, we had enough employees to take over the running of the business at the end of March.

We had calling cards made which we gave out at every opportunity, and Teresa designed a uniform for us with three S's sewn onto the breast pocket.

Phineas helped to facilitate our position in the community by introducing us to businessmen well connected in Boston society. Most of this was done at the Atwood and Bacon Oyster House.

He showed us parts of Boston we would never have found on our own. After a time, people accepted us, despite our Irish brogue.

21st March 1842

An enlivened Phineas arrived at the boarding house as we were eating our breakfast.

"Ebenezer and his daughter are arriving this evening. The Britannia was sighted in Halifax a few days ago," he said.

"Wonderful news. I wonder if Rebecca and her

family are on board?" asked Patrick.

"Who's Rebecca?" asked Phineas.

"Just a girl I met in Liverpool. She's supposed to be arriving with her family in March."

"Just a girl? It's the love of his life," I said.

"They'll probably be on it because the next one doesn't arrive until April," said Phineas.

My brother and I spent the rest of the day looking at offices near the Long Wharf. We found one on Broad Street that suited our requirements, so we signed a contract and paid a small deposit.

Things were moving far quicker than expected, and we'd already received a few enquiries from small businesses in the area.

At sunset on that calm spring evening, the Britannia arrived and docked at the Long Wharf.

My brother and I were waiting with Phineas when Patrick spotted Rebecca. She was standing on the deck with Kathleen, and they were both waving frantically.

"There they are! They must have met on the journey!" he yelled.

Ebenezer was the first off, followed by a hoard of passengers.

He spoke to Phineas for a few minutes, then headed towards us.

"It's so nice to be on solid ground again," he said.

"How was the journey?" I asked.

"Rough, but not as rough as yours. The captain told me all about it."

"I see Kathleen and Rebecca are acquainted," said Patrick.

"Yes, they've been inseparable since they met in the ladies saloon. What a lovely family. Her father, Michael, told us how you prevented him from falling down the cellar. These acts of kindness are becoming a habit. Is everything okay here?"

"Yes, fine. We've got a lot to tell you," said Patrick.

"Phineas will bring me up-to-date tonight. We can discuss things in the morning after breakfast. Can you be at my house by ten?"

"Yes, we can. We've had calling cards made for the security business," I said, handing him one of ours.

"I see you've wasted no time. That's what I like to see."

Kathleen and Rebecca walked towards us with Michael and his wife trailing behind. Rebecca ran into Patrick's arms and hugged him passionately.

Kathleen and I looked at each other awkwardly, then I kissed her hand, more formally.

"Welcome to Boston," I said, bowing my head.

"Thank you, and I look forward to showing you around."

"I'm meeting with your father in the morning. Maybe after, we could go for a walk around the common."

"That would be nice. I shall look forward to it."

My brother and I greeted Rebecca's parents, then much to our surprise, Michael produced a small bag from his pocket.

"This is for you two. It's your winnings from The Grand Liverpool Steeplechase. There's a pound's worth in dollars. We got 9 to 1 in the end."

"Wow! Gaylad won?" I asked.

"Yes, Tom Olliver did a superb job riding him."

My brother and I linked arms and done a little jig in the street.

Ebenezer and Kathleen boarded their carriage and set off for Beacon Hill while my brother sorted out a carriage for Mick and his family.

"Where are you staying, Rebecca?" asked Patrick.

"Number 10 Howard Street for now, but once things are organized, we'll be living above the Green Dragon Tavern.

Can you call tomorrow when you've finished your business with Ebeneezer?"

"Of course I can. I know where it is. It's just around the corner from us."

"I'll see you tomorrow then," she said as the carriage pulled away.

22nd March 1842

The following morning, my brother and I made our way to Beacon Hill. The sun was shining, and spring was in the air.

Ebenezer's six-bedroomed redbrick row house looked luxurious with amazing views over Boston common.

The housekeeper, a stout woman with a stern countenance, showed us into the study. Ebenezer and Kathleen were sitting at a large desk in the library, awaiting our arrival.

"Can you bring them some tea please, Agnes?" asked Kathleen.

"Certainly, Mam," she replied.

"I'll leave you to it. Are we still on for our walk, Sean?"

"Yes, of course," I replied.

"Well, I'll see you later. I have a picnic to prepare," said Kath.

"Right, gentlemen. Let's get started. I've just been going over the contract that my solicitor's have drawn up regarding you taking over the security. It just needs your signature's then a year's money will be paid into your account. I've set the date for the transition as the 01st April if that's all right with you."

"That's fine. We have a business account at the bank under the company name, Safe and Sound Security. Francis Brown sorted it out for us," I said.

"That's perfect. Is there anything you want to discuss?"

We told him about the office in Broad Street and our plans to expand in the future.

"That's good. You need an office if you want people to take you seriously. I can introduce you to a few people, but be warned, they don't look favourably towards Catholics."

"We've already been warned about that, so we're thinking of converting to Protestantism."

"I don't blame you. I remember a riot in 1837 on the very street your office is in. It's known as the Broad Street Riot:

Volunteer firefighters, who were all working-class Protestants, had just finished putting a fire out in Roxbury. They stopped off at a saloon to wash away the smoke.

On the way back to the station, they found the road blocked by an Irish Catholic Funeral Parade. One fireman began cursing the mourners and pushed one of them. A melee broke out that quickly escalated.

Paving stones were hurled, and makeshift weapons appeared, including the brigades fire axes. The firemen ran to the station and rang a bell that called out the other fire brigade's in the city, but by the time they got there, the funeral had passed. The firefighters then attacked the crowd that had gathered. Over a thousand people on each side engaged in battle. No one was known to be killed, but the fighting went on for hours. That's the type of prejudice you could be up against."

"Well, if that's not a compelling reason, nothing is. Is it something you could help us with?" asked Patrick.

"I attend the Old North Church on Salem Street. I'll have a word with the rector, Reverend John Woart, and see what he has to say. It would certainly open doors for you."

The maid arrived and placed a tray of tea on the desk.

Ebenezer poured while I told him about our horrendous journey to Boston and how Teresa had diffused a precarious situation in Halifax.

"That doesn't surprise me somehow. Teresa is a very astute woman with a knack for problem solving.

Phineas told me about Oliver and Sarah and how Charles Smithers encouraged them to steal. He must be like his grandfather. I didn't like him very much, as you know, although, I don't like to speak ill of the dead."

"Dead! When did that happen?" I asked.

"About a month ago, I think. My coachman Eugene found out about it when he went to visit his sister."

"That explains a lot. We heard that Charles had gone back to Ireland on business," said Patrick.

"Before you go, I have a letter for you, Sean. Father Sullivan gave it to me."

I took the letter off him and placed it in my coat pocket to read later.

"It's probably from your Esteemed Friend," said Patrick.

"It is, I recognise the writing," I replied.

Chapter 16

After our meeting, Patrick went off to rendezvous with Rebecca. He walked down the road with a spring in his step. I'd never seen him looking so happy.

Kathleen and I began our walk around the common. She looked elegant in a stunning dress in shades of brown and blue and made by a professional seamstress. It had a long-waisted bodice, tight narrow sleeves and a domed shaped skirt that skimmed the floor as she walked. Her bonnet matched perfectly with the blue of her dress.

She held onto my arm with the familiarity of a close acquaintance, and my heart skipped a beat. On her other arm, she held a basket of food.

"I see you've come prepared," I said.

"Yes, I thought a picnic would be nice, seeing as the sun is shining."

We passed Nannies pushing babies in perambulators, courting couples strolling arm in arm and families laden with food.

Many demure looking women held parasols to maintain their pale complexions.

Young girls played a game called graces and threw hoops back and fore to each other, attempting to catch the hoop on a rod.

The boys were more boisterous, doing handstands and cartwheels and climbing trees.

"I love this place. It's like an oasis amidst the

hustle and bustle of the city," she said.

"I've resisted the temptation to walk around it. I was waiting to share the experience with you. You seemed to know a lot about it when we spoke in your father's library."

"It's just things I've read about over the years. The townsfolk purchased it off a settler in 1634 and used it as a common grazing area. It continued that way until 1830, but then cows were banned due to overgrazing."

"Is that a graveyard on the far side?"

"Yes, It's the Central Burying Ground. That came a bit later.

The British Redcoats had an encampment here for many years. It's hard to imagine when you look at the place now."

We reached the centre of the common where I saw the biggest Elm tree I'd ever seen. It must have been at least seventy feet high.

"Wow! That's enormous, and it looks so majestic," I said.

"It's known by the locals as the Hanging Tree. Do you remember me mentioning the dark side of the common? Well, this is it."

"What do you mean?"

"In the not so distant past, public executions took place here. When the tree became too old and weak to support hangings, they constructed gallows next to it.

Witches, pirates, murderers, thieves, Indians and Quakers have all been hanged here over the centuries.

The Boston martyrs saw their end here in 1660, just for their religious beliefs.

They built whipping posts and stocks to punish criminals, and later, many were executed by firing squad."

"It's hard to believe when you look at it today: Families picnicking and children playing without a care in the world," I said.

"Yes, you're right. It is hard to believe."

"Where do they hang people now?"

"In the South of Boston. I'm not sure where exactly, and I don't particularly want to know."

We walked through an avenue of trees to a spot far away from the giant Elm and set a small blanket on the grass. Spring flowers were showing signs of life, poking their heads above ground in search of sunlight.

We ate chicken and bread and sat in silence, enjoying the tranquillity.

I remembered the letter and took it out of my pocket.

"A letter from your parents?" asked Kath.

"No, It's from a friend of mine named Boz. He's a well known author. We've been writing to each other for many years."

I told her about our fortuitous meeting in Liverpool, our journey together to America and Boz's reasons for coming.

"I've never heard of him. Is he still here?"

"No, he's back in England now."

I read the letter to myself, then gave Kath a brief account of its contents.

"He states that he loved Boston but wasn't overly keen on the rest of his trip. Multitudes followed him everywhere, and he found many people overbearing, boastful, vulgar, uncivil, insensitive and above all inquisitive. Those making money from his name, and the disgusting habit of tobacco spitting in the street, disgusted him."

"I don't think he'll be back in a hurry then," said Kath.

"Who knows? You may be right."

"My father told me about the children, Oliver and Sarah. I think it's wonderful what you've done. I can't imagine what life would be like on the streets at such a tender age."

"They're good kids. They just needed a chance in life like what your father did for us."

"You earned that through an act of kindness. They could have killed my father that day if it wasn't for you. Many people walked past and chose not to get involved. You didn't though."

"When are you going to work on the farm in Concord?" I asked.

"Next week, probably. I won't be working full time. I plan to spend my weekends here in Boston with my father.

"Who owns it? Is it Phineas's brother?"

"Yes, his name is Arthur. They're both Quakers and abolitionists and do a lot to help the cause."

"Do they? Well, I didn't know that," I said.

"Phineas is a member of the Boston Vigilance Committee. They protect the escaped slaves that arrive here by land and sea. Many of them arrive as stowaways on coastal trading vessels while others arrive through the Underground Railroad or the Freedom Train."

"I've heard of the Underground Railroad. What is it exactly?"

"It's a network of secret routes and safe houses to help slaves escape from the south into the free states of the north, then on into Canada. There are also routes to Mexico and overseas."

"They're involved in that?"

"Yes, and their parents before them. When I used to stay there, people would come and go at the strangest of hours.

One night, Arthur caught me spying on them. He took me to one side and explained everything in detail.

They use railroad terminology to hide their true purpose. A safe house is a station, and the owner a station master. Conductors are guides who help them on their way, and escapees are known as passengers or cargo. I've acted as a conductor occasionally. It's dangerous, but I couldn't sit back and do nothing. Most of them head for Canada where slavery has been abolished. They call it the Promised Land.

He told me about the federal marshalls, bounty hunters and slave catchers that hunt down runaways with impunity. Sometimes they even capture free slaves and take them back to the south.

Phineas's house here in Boston is a station. Their actions have helped thousands of people over the years, and I've nothing but admiration for them."

"I've never understood slavery. To deprive someone of their basic rights is inhumane," I said.

"I agree, wholeheartedly. I just hope that things improve in the future. Do you think you'll ever return to Ireland?"

"I don't think so. There aren't many opportunities there for me, but who knows what the future holds.

Our business here is doing well at the moment, thanks to your father's connections, and we've plenty of room for expansion."

We sat there for hours talking, and the chemistry between us was almost tangible.

I went to bed that night, but sleep eluded me. I couldn't stop thinking about her.

I'd marry her one day; of that, I was sure.

Chapter 17

Over the next three years, our business prospered, and the future was looking good.

Phineas moved into the boarding-house after marrying Mary in September 1843.

In the same year, James and Teresa bought the drapery and menswear store off Ebenezer. Both parties were happy with the outcome. Ebenezer had bought the place for next to nothing and made a handsome profit.

Rebecca stopped working for her parents and took over the running of our office in Broad Street. She had enough of serving drunken sailors and dealing with their lewd remarks.

Patrick and Rebecca married in September 1844 and bought a house on Beacon Hill.

I still lived in Hawkins Street, saving every penny I earned.

Patrick and I converted to Protestantism and were welcomed with open arms at the Old North Church.

The rail networks were expanding, and the industrial revolution was in full flow. In December 1844, we'd secured a lucrative contract with the Boston Manufacturing Company that owned textile mills throughout New England.

Kathleen and I spent all of our spare time together, and our feelings for each other grew with each passing day.

Ebenezer, forever a creature of habit, spent his

summers in Boston and his winters in Cork.

15ᵗʰ *October 1845*

It was the opening night of Murphy's Tavern, near Bunker Hill, Charlestown.

Mick and Carolina had achieved their ambition of owning a tavern and stood proudly behind the bar, greeting their guests.

We were all there apart from Ebenezer who'd returned to Cork.

"I think they'll do well here," said Patrick, deep in conversation with James.

"Yes, I agree. It's in a good location, near the monument. They'll probably get a lot of passing trade."

The monument was a 211 foot obelisk, built entirely from quarried granite and dedicated to Dr Joseph Warren who fell at the battle of Bunker Hill at the start of the American Revolutionary War. It was officially opened in 1842, after many years of planning and fundraising.

Phineas was in a befuddled state having drunk his fair share of whisky. At one stage, he attempted an Irish Jig and fell over repeatedly, sending us into fits of laughter.

There was much singing and merriment, and the atmosphere was convivial.

It all changed when Charles Smithers walked in accompanied by two seafaring men of dubious character. One of them was tall and muscular like

Patrick, while the other was smaller in stature. Both had the tattoo of an anchor on their right hand.

The atmosphere changed within seconds, and the room went quiet. My brother and I looked at each other knowingly.

"Here comes trouble," I said.

"Yes, I think you're right going by what Mick told me earlier. He said that Charles has offered to buy the place at way below the market value. He's refused of course. I think Charles is worried about the competition," said Patrick.

"James? Can you take the girls into the back room? It may get ugly in here soon," I said.

"No problem," he replied.

Charles sat down in the corner out of the way while his thugs went about their work. It didn't take long to get a reaction out of someone, and that someone was me.

The bigger one slapped me across the back as I took a gulp of my Guinness. I didn't want Mick's furniture to get damaged, so I said, "If you're looking for a fight, let's step outside."

When we got to the street, I squared up to him but the smaller one took a swing at me. I ducked and countered with a punch to his jaw.

"Two against one, is it?" said my brother, taking his jacket off.

The bigger one caught him off guard with a glancing blow, but Patrick replied with a few punches of his own, knocking him to the floor.

I was getting the better of the smaller one until

he drew a knife from his waistband. The crowd of onlookers stepped back in fright as the blade shimmered under the gaslight. I was afraid for my life, but Mick saved the day by striking the man's wrist with a cosh. The knife fell to the floor, and Mick kicked it away. He then turned his attention towards Mick, but before he could react, I caught him with a right hook that landed perfectly on his temple. His legs wobbled underneath him, and he collapsed to the floor in a heap.

Patrick and the taller one continued to exchange punches, but my brother was getting the upper hand. Patrick eventually knocked him out with a punch to the jaw.

"Thanks, Mick," I said.

"Your welcome. I always keep a cosh behind the bar. I'm glad I thought to pick it up."

Mick walked towards Charles Smithers, his temper rising with every step. We could hear his voice booming from across the room as he gave Charles a piece of his mind. I sat next to Kath and listened with interest.

"Keep your thugs out of my pub!"

"They're not my thugs. I've never seen them before!" yelled Charles.

"I saw you speaking to them earlier!"

"They asked me for directions to the monument! There's no crime in that!"

"Drink your drink, and don't come in here again!"

"I wouldn't want to with the type of clientele

you have. I'd rather drink in my tavern. It's far more civilised than this hell-hole."

Charles finished his drink and walked out with his head held aloof.

"Arrogant bastard," said Patrick, downing his pint.

The party atmosphere soon returned, and we continued drinking until the early hours.

16th October 1845

The following morning, my brother and I were rougher than a blacksmiths file. At midday, we headed for the Atwood and Bacon Oyster House. We'd been hearing scuttlebutt from Ireland that the potato crop had failed, and we wanted to know if the rumours were true.

We were sitting at the bar enjoying a dish of oysters when John Hewitt walked in. He'd recently arrived from Ireland.

"What happened to you? You look like shit," he said.

I had a swollen right eye that was slowly turning black, and my brother had a few grazes on his left cheek.

Patrick gave him a blow by blow account of the previous night's shenanigans, including Charles Smithers's role in the proceedings.

"That bastard needs to be brought down a peg or two. He's an arrogant arsehole who thinks he's above the law," he said.

He ordered a Guinness and joined us. I asked him the question I was dreading the answer of:

"Have you heard about a potato blight in Ireland, John?"

"Yes, unfortunately, it's true. I was hoping to bump into you today as I have a letter from your parents," he said, handing it to me.

I opened it tentatively and read it out loud:

Dear Sean and Patrick,

I hope this letter finds you in good health and that your fortunes continue to prosper.

Your mother and sisters are well and send their love.

You may have already heard about the late blight that has struck Ireland and the annihilative effects it's had on our crops. I knew as early as August that something was wrong by the smell of rotting leaves that gravitated towards our home. Fifty per cent of the crop has failed, and next year could be even worse, but I hasten to add, Ebenezer has been our saviour once again.

He came to visit us this morning with an offer at the most opportune time. His housekeeper and her husband are retiring to a cottage they inherited in England.

He has asked us to take over the running of the house, which includes remuneration and accommodation for us and the girls.

Who would have thought that your actions on

the day of Rebecca's funeral would end up having
such a fundamental effect on our lives?

If you hadn't reacted to those cries of help from
Ebenezer, you'd still be here with us with nothing
to look forward to except a penurious life of hunger
and misery. Maybe Rebecca was looking out for us
that day.

I worry for our neighbours. Without money,
they'll be evicted and sent to the Workhouse.

I can only hope that Robert Peel and his
Government do something to help the Irish people.

Look out for each other and don't worry about
us, we're safe and well,

Love Da.

We both sighed with relief.

"Thank God for Ebenezer. I'll have to write to him this evening and thank him," I said.

Patrick nodded in agreement.

"I'll be returning to Ireland in a few days. I'll deliver the letter for you. Leave it behind the bar for me," said John.

"I'll do that, and thank you," I replied.

"Shall we have another? Hair of the Dog, whatever that means," said Patrick.

"It's short for hair of the dog that bit you. It comes from an old belief that someone bitten by a rabid dog could be cured of rabies by taking a potion containing some of the dog's hair," said John.

"Well, I hope this next potion of Guinness

cures me," said Patrick, laughing.

A few minutes later, Rebecca joined us, grinning from ear to ear.

"I thought I'd find you here. I've got some good news that couldn't wait."

"Do we have a new client?" asked Patrick.

"No, It's something more important than that," she said, dramatically.

"Well, don't keep us on tenterhooks! What is it!" he exclaimed.

"I'm pregnant!"

Patrick's mouth fell open in surprise. He held her in his arms and yelled: "I'm going to be a father!"

That evening, Patrick and I sat down and constructed two letters. One for Ebenezer, thanking him for everything, and the other for our parents informing them of Rebecca's pregnancy.

Chapter 18

16 months later

February 13th 1847

At 08:30 am, on a cold Saturday morning, the streets of Boston were full of life. Horse-drawn carts and handcarts delivered fresh produce to the stores along State Street. Ladies in fine bonnets and fashionable gentlemen in top hats mingled with seedy-looking sailors with ponytails. The eating houses were all busy, and the smell of sizzling bacon and freshly baked bread enhanced the appetite.

It had been raining throughout the night, so I walked with trepidation on the slippery cobbles.

I arrived at our office to find my brother with his feet up on the desk. He was reading a pamphlet and seemed engrossed. His wife had the weekend off and was at home with their ten-month-old baby, Patrick.

"What's that you're reading?" I asked.

"Phineas dropped it in earlier. It's something the Quakers are circulating all over the country. They're asking for donations of food and money to be sent to Ireland, and they've set up soup kitchens there to feed the hungry.

It state's that relief committees are being set up all over America, and people are responding. "

"Are they setting one up here? Maybe we can

help?"

"I don't know. You could ask Phineas later. He seems to know everything that goes on in the city."

We sat in the office for a while, waiting for the Britannia to arrive with news from back home. Since the famine started, tens of thousands of Irish had arrived in America. Many died during the journey from cholera and typhus, a situation exacerbated by the horrendous conditions and lack of proper food. They became known as coffin ships because of the high mortality rate. Stories abounded of predatory sharks following them, waiting for the dead to be thrown overboard.

We'd been told by many that the latest crops had failed again, compounded by the worst winter on record.

"Shall we head for the wharf? She'll be docking soon," said Patrick.

"Yes, let's go."

When we arrived, Phineas was there with a team of stevedores, waiting to unload.

"Morning, Phineas. Are you expecting a big delivery?" I asked.

"Only Guinness. Ebenezer has refused to export food out of Ireland for obvious reasons."

"Good for him," I said. "It's a shame the British Government doesn't think the same way. There are still large quantities of livestock, butter and other produce being exported out of Ireland. How can they justify that when people are starving?"

"Yes, it beggars belief. I've heard stories of

starving Irishmen loading grain onto ships bound for Britain while the landowners and bureaucrats are enjoying lavish meals."

"I need to speak to you. Will you be in your office later?"

"Yes, I'll be there shortly."

My brother and I couldn't believe our eyes when we saw the mass of emaciated bodies about to disembark: children with sunken eyes and hollow cheeks and adults with misery etched upon their faces. They could barely walk. We'd never seen such despair. We'd heard the harrowing stories, but to witness this spectacle induced us to tears.

Their problems had only just begun. The locals looked down on them with disdain and viewed them as violent alcoholics. Jobs were scarce, and most of them had no skills apart from farming. I'd even seen jobs advertised in the papers stating, No Irish Need Apply.

"I'm sure that's Tim O'Brien and his family on the gangway!" yelled Patrick in disbelief.

"My god! The last time we saw him was on the steps outside the town hall in Skibb," I said.

A flicker of recognition showed on Tim's face when he saw us.

"Is that you, Patrick?" he inquired.

"Yes, it is. I didn't expect to see you. How are things back home?"

"A million times worse than you can ever imagine. The workhouse in Skibb is overwhelmed, and people are dying from disease and hunger wherever you look. There's a mass grave in Abbeystrewry Graveyard, and the bodies are piled high. We are the lucky ones. Father Sullivan found us on the street and paid for our fare."

My brother and I were lost for words. We'd heard the rumours, but to hear it firsthand left us heartbroken.

"Do you have money and somewhere to stay?" asked Patrick.

"No, we have neither. I need to find work as soon as possible."

"You can stay with us. My wife and I will be glad to have you, and don't worry about work; you need to build your strength up first."

"Did you hear that, Aoife? We can stay at Patrick's."

"Thank God for that. These kids have forgotten what it's like to have a full belly and a roof over their heads," she said, tearfully.

"Do you have any luggage, Tim?" asked Patrick.

"No, what you see is what we've got."

We took them to Phineas's office, and I made them hot tea while Patrick sorted out transport.

Phineas arrived as they were leaving.

"Who are they, Sean?" he asked.

"A family we know from Skibbereen. They're going to stay at Patrick's until they find something more permanent."

"They look so desperate. It makes you

appreciate what you've got."

"Perhaps they could stay at your place, seeing as you're living at the boarding house with Mary."

"That's not possible, I'm afraid. Mary and I are moving back in there soon. She's going to retire from the boarding house as soon as Ebenezer finds a replacement."

"I can't say I blame her. She's worked hard all her life. It would have been awkward anyway, especially if you had passengers or cargo arriving during the night."

He looked at me with a frown.

"You know about the Underground Railroad?"

"Yes, Kathleen told me about it. I admire what you do."

"Of course. She would have witnessed all sorts of comings and goings at my brother's farm. Have you ever stayed there?"

"It's funny you should ask that. Kathleen has invited me to stay there next weekend, with your brother's permission, of course."

"Good, I think you'll enjoy it. It's nice to get away from the city now and then."

"I'm looking forward to it. I've been stuck in Boston for too long."

"There were a lot of Irish onboard today. The most I've seen this week," said Phineas, changing the subject.

"Where are they all going to live?" I asked.

"Most of them are gravitating towards the East of Boston. The area is quickly becoming a slum with overcrowding and disease. How are things in Ireland? Did your friends say anything?"

"Yes, they did, and it's far worse than we thought. They need help desperately. Have you heard anything about a relief committee being set up?"

"I have. There's a meeting at Faneuil Hall next Thursday at two. The Mayor, Josiah Quincy Jnr, will chair it, and John Greenleaf Whittier, the famous poet and abolitionist, will be the keynote speaker.

President Polk and Vice President George Dallas had a public meeting in Washington DC recently and asked the people of America to help in any way they can.

Protestant Churches, Catholic Dioceses and Jewish Synagogues are all responding. Teas, concerts, balls and bazaars are being held all over the country to raise money. Even the Choctaw Indians are contributing. I heard that the Catholic Diocese in Boston has raised $20.000."

"Perhaps we can all go together? What do you think?" I asked.

"Sounds good to me. We can meet at the Atwood and Bacon Oyster House for lunch."

"Okay, I'll see you then, if not before."

I left Phineas to his work, then met up with Kathleen for our customary walk around the common.

Chapter 19

Thursday 18th February 1847

Patrick and I arrived at the Oyster House at one. Phineas, James and Mick arrived a few minutes later and joined us at the bar.

"How's Teresa?" I asked James.

"She's fine and the shops doing well. At the moment she's making clothes out of waste material to send to Skibbereen. The girls from the Lowell Textile Mills have been doing the same. Getting the stuff to Ireland is a problem though," said James.

Two dapper gentlemen walked in and headed towards us.

"Here comes some friends of mine that I'd like you to meet. This is Captain Robert Bennet Forbes and his brother, John. Their family have been merchants in the city for many years," said Phineas.

We all shook hands and introduced ourselves.

"We've got an idea we want to put to the committee," said Robert.

"What is it?" asked Phineas.

"It's quite simple, really. Instead of just sending money, we want to send food and clothing. Corn monopolists in Ireland are charging extortionist prices. We could send ours for one-third of the price."

"How would you get it there?" I asked.

"I want the committee to petition congress for

use of the warship USS Jamestown that's currently idle in the Charlestown Navy Yard. I would command it and seek a volunteer crew."

"That sounds like a good idea. If they agree, we could supply some men to help with the cargo," I said.

"I've already spoken to the Labourers Aid Society, and they've agreed to help with the loading, that's if our petition is successful, but the more the merrier."

"I could donate a few kegs of rum if that will help," said Mick.

"I'd volunteer myself Mick if it meant a free drink out of you," said Patrick, laughing.

We arrived at Faneuil Hall to a large gathering of people. Over four thousand had arrived from all over New England.

We found some space and listened closely as the mayor addressed the crowd and introduced the twenty-one committee members.

John Greenleaf Whittier spoke eloquently of the conditions in Ireland and pleaded for generosity. Others followed, each delivering a heartfelt message, beseeching everyone for action.

The speeches had the desired effect, and by the end of the meeting, the assembly dispersed, united in a common goal.

Captain Forbes and his brother said their goodbye's and went off to speak to the mayor.

Mick invited us to his tavern, but much to my brother's surprise, I declined.

He stared at me with a look of credulity.

"I've never known you to refuse a pint. What have you got on that's so important?" he asked.

"I have to go shopping."

"Shopping! Shopping for what?"

"You'll find out soon enough."

I walked away leaving my brother in a state of bewilderment.

Earlier that week, I had an epiphany. The precariousness of things in Ireland had hit home to me. I could wait for the perfect time, but the clock was ticking, and life was too short. I would propose to Kathleen on the weekend, and the farm in Concord would be the ideal place.

I headed for the jewellers on Washington Street, hoping that the ring I had in mind was still in the window. Kathleen had pointed it out every time we passed. If that wasn't a hint, nothing was. Much to my relief, the French Pave Diamond Engagement ring was still there, shining brightly. I purchased it at a reasonable price and headed home.

The night before my trip to Concord, I slept fitfully. I kept going over the proposal in my head, envisioning all sorts of irrational scenarios. Eventually, I drifted off to sleep with a plan in mind.

Saturday 20th February 1847

The following morning, I ate a hearty breakfast and made my way outside.

Ebenezer's carriage, drawn by two beautifully manicured black horses, was waiting for me. The coachman hopped down with athleticism that belied his barrel waist and introduced himself.

"William Dyer, at your service. Sean MacCarthy, I believe?"

"Yes, it is. Pleased to meet you, William."

I boarded, sat down next to him and placed my small overnight bag on the floor beneath my feet. William handed me a blanket.

"It's not too bad at the moment, Sean, but it's a lot colder inland. You can pull the hood over if you want. We should be in Concord by ten with a bit of luck."

I had considered taking the Fitchburg train from Charlestown which stopped off at Concord on the way but decided against it. By carriage, I could enjoy the scenery and stop off somewhere en route.

We travelled through Charlestown via the Charles River Bridge and before long, we were in the countryside.

It was nice to escape the city and feel the fresh air on my face. I felt invigorated.

My mind drifted, and I thought of Paul Revere and his famous midnight ride to Concord at the start of the American Revolution. The British troops were on the march in search of Revolutionary leaders and military stores.

Along with his compatriot, William Dawes, they warned the militia. The following day, the first military engagement of the war took place at Lexington and Concord.

"Have you been there before?" asked William.

"Not the town itself, but my brother and I have been to many of the textile mills and factories in the area. We own a security company and have contracts with many of them."

The frost in the surrounding fields thawed as the winter sun broke through the clouds. Despite this, it was cold. I did the buttons up on my winter coat and wrapped the blanket around my shoulders.

We stopped occasionally to allow farmers to pass, their oxen driven carts overflowing with produce for the Boston markets and stores.

We passed farms and wooden balloon framed houses, but what surprised me the most were the many groundbreaking innovations on show.

Many used the ingenious steel plough, invented by John Deere, that revolutionised farming.

We passed fish-filled rivers, woods teeming with game and fertile soil that stretched for miles across the meadowlands.

As we neared Nashua and Nashville, the scenery changed. Water powered textile mills owned by the Nashua Manufacturing Company took over the landscape. Railroads linked them to

Boston, bringing wealth and prosperity to the town and employment for many.

We stopped for refreshment at a tavern overlooking the Nashua River, then continued on our way.

We arrived at Concord, the first inland settlement in the Massachusetts Bay Colony, a little earlier than expected.

There were solid looking craft shops lining the streets that housed clockmakers, cabinetmakers, hatters, blacksmiths and pencil makers. They all manufactured items for local sale and export. The town was a hub of trade with a thriving community.

"That's the new railway station," said William as we passed Walden Pond. "It's the line that runs from Boston to Fitchburg."

I glanced over to see a crowd of people waiting patiently for the train to arrive.

We left the town behind us, and after a few miles, entered a wooded area that was being cleared.

"They're making room for new mills and factories. They're sprouting up everywhere," said William.

"It's the price we pay for progress, I suppose," I replied.

Not long after, we arrived at a wooden framed entranceway with the legend **Welcome to Finn's Farm,** emblazoned across the top.

Chapter 20

Two barking dogs of undetermined breed followed us down a dirt track road that led to a two-storey farmhouse with wide columned porches. Two post and beam barns stood to the left of it and a smaller property for guests, to the right.

Kathleen was outside with the Finn family, waving excitedly.

I jumped down from the carriage and hugged her tightly.

"This is Sean, everyone!" she yelled.

I shook hands with them all: Arthur, his wife Anne and their three sons. The oldest son Luke was sixteen, followed by John and Michael, aged ten and twelve respectively.

Arthur had the same intense sapphire blue eyes as his brother, but a build and height similar to mine. His boys had the same look except for the youngest, Michael. He was tall for his age and had brown eyes like his mother.

"Thank you for the invite, Mr Finn. I've heard so much about you off Kathleen."

"It's my pleasure, and please call me Arthur. We've been looking forward to meeting you. How was the journey?"

"I quite enjoyed it. It's so nice to get away from the city and feel the fresh air on my face. I've missed the open space and the sounds of nature."

"I bet. I don't think I could live in a city."

"I'm beginning to feel that way myself. I grew

up on a farm in Ireland, so I'm used to the outdoors."

"Come on in and make yourself at home," said Anne. "I've water boiling for tea."

Anne was a small woman, as wide as she was tall.

I entered the farmhouse to the smell of fresh bread that baked in the wood-burning oven. A kettle boiled on the centre ring while a pot of stew simmered gently beside it.

A large oak dining table, big enough for at least twelve people, stood next to a window that overlooked the farm. Next to that, a comfortable living area opened onto a passageway that led to a washroom and a well ventilated dairy.

"What a cosy home you have," I said.

"Thank you. My grandparents built it, but it's been renovated a few times since then," said Arthur.

Anne poured the tea while the rest of us sat around the table. Kathleen sat next to me and held my hand affectionately.

"I'll be travelling back with you tomorrow. My father's due to arrive on Monday, and I want to be there to meet him," she said.

"It's a bit early for him, isn't it?"

"Yes, it is. He wants to help the people in Ireland, and he thinks he's best suited to do that from here."

"That's typical of your father. I've never met a more altruistic person in my life. Does he know about the relief committee?"

"I doubt it. He'll probably get involved knowing him."

"When you've drunk your tea, I'll show you around the farm," said Arthur.

"Thank you. I can't wait to see it."

"Luke! Take a cup of tea out to William! He'll be making his way back once the horses are fed and watered!" yelled Anne, who was taking the bread out of the oven.

"Yes, Mother, and there's no need to shout. I'm not deaf."

"How's the business doing, Sean?" asked Arthur.

"Very well. We seem to have a system that works well for us. My brother, Patrick, deals with the new clients. He seems to have a knack for it. I deal with the employment side of things while my sister-in-law keeps the finances in order."

"I'm so glad you're doing well. The new arrivals haven't been so lucky though, or so I hear."

"That's right. Many have been ostracised for their religious beliefs. People seem to think that all Irish Catholics are violent alcoholics and not worth employing."

"Let's hope that things improve in the future," said Arthur.

After our tea, Arthur showed me around the farm and gave me a brief history of his family:

"When my grandparents ran the farm, they were self-sufficient, growing enough to live on, but my parents improved on that by selling their produce to local markets.

We've improved on that again by purchasing the adjacent farm and supplying the textile mills with their dairy products and vegetables. They have a large workforce to feed. We now have 200 acres of rolling hills to utilise.

We've diversified in recent years, breeding our own livestock and investing in modern machinery."

I nodded as we walked until we came to a property at the back of the main house. It had a stable and a blacksmith's attached to it.

"I didn't see this on the way in," I said.

"It's for the farmhands we employ. It's basic, but at least they can live independently. We've got two hands living there at the moment, but a lot more during harvest."

"Kath told me about the farm, but I didn't realise how big it was."

"I believe she told you about our role as a station and the passengers we receive?"

"Yes, she did. I have great respect for the work you do. No one should be treated as chattel and valued as one would value an animal."

"Most of us in this area think like that, but we have to be careful because you never know who's listening. For some lowlifes, capturing slaves has become a lucrative business. Some slave owners from the south advertise a reward in the local papers. It doesn't help matters."

"Are you expecting anyone tonight?"

"No, they would have informed me by now. It's probably someone else's turn."

That afternoon, Kath and I had some time on our own. Luke saddled two horses for us, and we went for a ride. I hadn't ridden for a while, and it showed. Kath laughed when I nearly fell off, but I soon got into the swing of things.

In the evening, we had beef stew, chunks of bread and homemade apple pie. It was a simple meal but delicious nonetheless.

I got more and more nervous as I thought about my proposal. I planned to ask her on the porch of the guest house, beneath a full moon and a star speckled sky. It would be the perfect place.

After our meal, we chatted with the Finn family in front of a roaring fire in the living area.

I told them about the meeting at Faneuil Hall and Captain Forbes's idea of using one of the government's warships to transport food to Ireland.

"That's a brilliant idea. Let's hope the government agrees," said Arthur.

"We're at war with Mexico at the moment, so who knows?" said Luke.

We talked for a while until Arthur yawned. It triggered a chain reaction through the whole family.

"I think it's time we went to bed. The Quakers are holding a Friends Meeting tomorrow on State Street in Concord. We have a small service, and newcomers are always welcome. Would you like to accompany us? It's on your way. Luke will take you both to Boston afterwards," said Arthur.

"Yes, I'd love that," I replied.

The butterflies in my stomach did a merry dance as Kath and I walked to the guest house. We passed the kennels on our way, and the dogs wagged their tails in welcome.

"Good boy, George. Good boy, Washington. Go to sleep now," said Kath, soothingly.

"George and Washington, after the first American president. An excellent choice of names," I said.

I stepped onto the porch and opened the door. Its hinges creaked loudly from lack of use.

"Nobody has stayed here for a while. Arthur doesn't like to have guests because of his work with the Underground Railroad. He doesn't want to compromise anyone."

"That's understandable."

We entered a small living area that was cosy and warm. Arthur had lit a fire that burned brightly and was adequate for the size of the room. A small cabinet stood against one wall, supporting a jug of water and two glasses. A door at the side led to two adjoining bedrooms and a washroom.

I placed my overnight bag in the first bedroom, then joined Kath on the porch.

"It's a bit chilly. I'll get us a blanket each," she said.

I sat in one of the two rocking chairs and looked up at the full moon. It shone brightly, and the stars sparkled like diamonds. *This is perfect. What could go wrong?* I thought.

Chapter 21

At close to midnight, I plucked up the courage and rose out of my chair.

"Where are you going?" she asked.

"Nowhere, there's something I need to ask you."

I dropped to one knee, and as I did so, the dogs barked ferociously.

"There's something wrong," said Kath. "They rarely bark like that."

She sprang from her chair, knocking me over in the process.

I couldn't believe it. Of all the times to bark, it had to be now.

Arthur came out of the main house carrying a lantern.

"What's wrong?" he yelled.

"Don't know! The dogs are behaving strangely. They should be used to the noises at night!" yelled Kath.

We walked to the main house and joined Arthur on the terrace. We all stood there, listening intently.

"I just heard something coming from that way," said Kath, pointing to the dirt track road and the main entrance.

"Come with me, Sean. We'll take a closer look," said Arthur.

We walked together, holding the lantern out in front of us. It was pitch black, despite the moonlight.

As we neared the entranceway, I could see two pairs of eyes shining in the dark.

"Who goes there!" I shouted.

"Mr Finn? The conductor sent us. The Wayside House in Concord is too dangerous. The slave catchers are watching it," came a deep male voice.

"It's okay," replied Arthur. "I'm Mr Finn. We'll take care of you."

The two slaves walked nervously towards us, their eyes wide open in panic. The sweat on their ebony skin glistened in the light from the lantern.

The one doing the talking was tall, muscular, and looked about eighteen years of age. The other was slightly younger.

"My name is Abraham, and this is my younger brother Daniel."

"Are the slave catchers following you?" asked Arthur.

"No, the conductor warned us before we got too close. He gave us directions to this place."

"Follow me. We have a room behind the main house where you'll be safe. My wife will give you some food and water."

By the time we got back to the main house, Kath had calmed the dogs down. Anne gave Abraham and his brother some of the stew she had leftover, and before long, they were safely ensconced into their temporary home.

I returned to the porch of the guest house where Kath was waiting, grinning from ear to ear.

"I believe you were going to ask me something before we were rudely interrupted," she said, giggling.

"Yes, I was, but I can't remember what," I replied, scratching my head.

We both looked at each other then I started tapping my pockets with my right hand. My left was behind my back, holding the little box that contained the ring.

"My God! I can't find it. I must have dropped it somewhere."

"Sean MacCarthy! I'm going to kill you one of these days! Now finish the job!"

I opened the little box then dropped to one knee in front of her.

"Kathleen Foley. Will you do me the honour of being my wife?"

"Yes, of course. What took you so long?"

I pushed the ring onto her finger and kissed her passionately.

"I was waiting until I had enough money to buy us a farm in Ireland. I know that's what you aspire to, but it's difficult. I'd have enough if I sold my share of the business to Patrick, but it's out of the question at the moment. Maybe in a few years, things will be different."

"It doesn't matter to me, Sean. I don't care where we live as long as we're together."

"Then I think it's time for a toast."

"With what?"

I walked into the house and got a bottle of

Champagne from my bag and two glasses off the cabinet.

"Where did you get that from?"

"Us MacCarthy's always come prepared," I said, laughing.

I opened the bottle, sending the cork flying into the sky and filled the glasses to the brim.

"A toast: here's to us and a bright future," I said.

"What a waste this would have been if I'd said no."

"I would have used it to drown my sorrows," I replied.

That night was the first night we slept together. We made love passionately and fell asleep in each other's arms.

Sunday 21st February 1847

The following morning, we washed quickly in freezing cold water and joined the Finn's for breakfast.

They were all sitting around the big table, dressed in their Sunday best. Anne was cooking and wore an apron to protect her clothes.

"Good morning. Take a seat, breakfast won't be long," she said.

"What an eventful night we had," said Arthur.

"Yes, in more ways than one," replied Kath, laughing.

They all looked at her quizzically, then Kath

stood up and banged her fork on the table.

"Ladies and gentlemen! Last night Sean proposed to me! I am now engaged to be married!"

They all looked at us in surprise.

"Congratulations! When's the big day?" asked Anne.

"We haven't decided yet," I replied.

We all hugged each other, then Anne served us breakfast. She asked Luke to take some down to Abraham and Daniel along with a change of clothes.

When we'd finished, Kathleen helped Anne with the dishes while the boys went off to ready the carriages. We needed two: one for Luke to take us to Boston and another for the Finn's.

I joined Arthur, who was enjoying a cigar on the porch

"This is my Sunday treat. Would you like one?"

"No, thank you, Arthur. What's going to happen to the passengers?"

"They'll be travelling with you. Phineas will be expecting them. The carriage you're using has a box on the back. They'll fit inside it with room to spare."

"What about the meeting?"

"You could still go for a while and meet some of Kath's friends, but I'd forego the service if I was you. The sooner you're on your way, the better. What do you think?"

"I'll be glad to help."

A few minutes later, the boys arrived with the carriages and pulled up outside. Arthur explained the situation to Abraham and Daniel, and they climbed into the storage area willingly.

We set off at a steady clip and sat in silence until we reached Lexington.

"Do you know much about the Revolutionary War, Sean?" asked Kath.

"Only what I've read. I know the Colonists weren't happy with the new acts brought in by the British Government: the increased taxes and the fact that they had no representation in Parliament."

"This is where it all began. As the sun was rising in Lexington, they fired the first shots. Eight militia and one British soldier were killed. The militia fell back, and the 100 British regulars proceeded on to Concord.

When they arrived at the North Bridge, approximately 400 Minutemen were waiting for them. The Minutemen were civilian colonists, self-trained in weaponry and tactics. They were known for being ready at a minute's notice, hence the name.

There were casualties on both sides. The regulars fell back and joined the main body of the British forces.

More militia arrived from surrounding towns, and eventually, they drove the British back to Charlestown. Then they blockaded the city, starting the Siege of Boston."

Chapter 22

When we arrived at the meeting house, the sun broke through the clouds. It was still bitter cold, and I was glad of my winter coat. Kath wrapped her shawl around her shoulders then I helped her down from the carriage.

"Let's mingle. I'll introduce you to the Alcott's. They're abolitionists like us and a lovely family. Their second oldest daughter, Louisa May, who's only fifteen, is very interesting to talk to. Even at her age, she has very strong views on abolitionism, women's suffrage and social reform. She's an aspiring writer, and I think she's going to be famous one day."

Louisa's face lit up when she saw Kath.

"Kathleen! How nice to see you again."

"Good morning, everyone," said Kath, addressing the whole family. "This is my fiancé, Sean MacCarthy."

They all shook my hand warmly.

"Fiancé? When are you getting married?" asked Louisa.

"We're not sure. He only proposed to me last night."

We stood chatting for a while, then Arthur approached me with a worried expression on his face.

"I see you've met the Alcott's. Have you spoken to the father, Amos?"

"Only briefly. He seems a very amiable man," I

replied.

"They live at the Wayside, just down the road."

"Isn't that where the runaways were heading last night?"

"Yes, it was. I've spoken to Amos about it. He said that three riders had been watching the house all day. They were weather-beaten and wore duster long coats. The slave owners probably hired them to be this far north. They get paid for their time, so they don't care how far they travel. There's no sign of them at the moment, but I think it's best if you leave."

Kath and I headed back to the carriage. We made ourselves comfortable, covering our legs with a blanket. Luke picked up the reins, clicked his tongue, and we were soon on our way.

The town was peaceful with it being a Sunday, apart from a few people outside Wright's Tavern, who were boarding a stagecoach.

We passed through Nashua and Nashville, arriving in Boston at midday.

Phineas was standing outside when we pulled up, keen to get the passengers in and out of sight.

Between the four of us, we carried the box into the house.

When we were safe from prying eyes, Kath opened it. Abraham and Daniel stared up at us nervously.

"Everything is fine. You're in safe hands," said Phineas, reassuring them.

"Any problems on the way, Kath?" he asked.

"No, the roads were quiet."

She then recounted the previous night's activities and included my comical proposal. Phineas looked at me and giggled.

"I'm sorry for laughing. I can picture you kneeling there and Kath pushing you over."

"I felt like a right idiot. It wasn't one of my finest moments," I said.

"Never mind. At least she said yes."

Phineas and I took Abraham and his brother to a room upstairs. It was sparsely furnished with four single beds, a medium-sized table, four chairs and a washstand. A jug of water and four tankards stood on the table.

"You'll be staying here tonight, so make yourselves comfortable. I'll bring you some food later. Tomorrow you'll continue with the next stage of your journey," said Phineas.

"Thank you. We appreciate everything you're doing for us," replied Abraham, the more talkative of the two.

"Help yourselves to some water, and I'll see you later."

We returned downstairs, and I joined Kath and Luke at the dining table. Phineas went off to make coffee.

"Do you want me to drop you off at Beacon Hill?" asked Luke.

"No, we'll walk. It's not far, and we haven't much luggage," said Kath.

"Great, once I've had my coffee, I'll be on my

way," he said.

As Phineas returned with our drinks, there was a knock on the front door.

"I wonder who that could be? I don't normally have visitors on a Sunday," he said.

He opened the door to find Patrick standing there with a bleak expression on his face.

"Come in, Patrick. I was just pouring coffee."

As soon as I saw him, I knew something was wrong.

"I have some terrible news," he said. "Rebecca's father was murdered last night."

"Murdered? What happened?" I asked.

"After closing time, he went out to the back alley to open the gate ready for the night soil men to remove the excrement. Carolina heard a noise and went out to investigate. She found him on the floor in a pool of blood. He said he was set upon by the two pugnacious men who were causing trouble on the opening night. The ones we were fighting with.

Apparently, Charles Smithers has been using intimidation tactics to pressurise Mick into selling. He probably sent his heavies around to persuade him."

"That's going to be difficult to prove unless they catch the two men involved," said Phineas.

"The police and the night watch have a description of them. There can't be many men out there with a tattoo of an anchor on their right hand. They're probably long gone by now, but we do know one thing: there were no ships sailing last night so they're still in the country at least."

"So, Mick was conscious when Carolina found him?" asked Kath.

"Yes, but not for long. Some passersby stopped to help, but his wounds were too severe, and he bled to death. She's at our house at the moment with Rebecca and Tim's family."

"We'd better go there. They'll need our support," said Kath.

When we arrived, Carolina was sitting in the parlour with her daughter. They were both distraught and overcome with a mixture of grief and anger. Kath hugged them while I stood there, at a loss for words.

"Someone has to do something about that man. He can't get away with it," said Carolina, with tears rolling down her face.

"Don't worry, Mother. He won't get away with it. He'll have his comeuppance if it's the last thing I do," said Rebecca.

"What am I going to do with the tavern? I can't run it on my own."

"Don't worry about that. We'll sort something out in the future. Let's just concentrate on giving Mick the send off he deserves," said Patrick.

Which was exactly what we did. We laid his body out in the parlour at my brother's house and arranged the funeral for four days' time.

Monday 21st February 1847

The following morning, Kath and I headed for the Long Wharf to meet Ebenezer.

On the way, we stopped off at the Bell in Hand on Union Street. It was once owned by the cities last town crier, Jimmy Wilson. We ordered two mugs of its famous ale that I'd heard so much about and sat at a table by the window.

The proprietor brought it over, and it didn't disappoint. It was so thick they had to serve it in two mugs, one for the ale and one for the froth.

"I'm a bit nervous about meeting your father. I have to give him bad news first, then ask him for his daughter's hand in marriage. It doesn't seem right, somehow," I said.

"Don't worry. It'll be fine. I'll tell him about Mick's death. You can ask him for my hand in marriage when we're back at the house. My father's not an ogre. He's been expecting you to propose for a long time."

"He has?"

"Yes, of course. He's dropped hints often enough. I think he wants grandchildren."

"I didn't realise that. I don't feel so bad now."

We finished our ale, wandered around Quincy Market, then headed for the wharf. We joined Phineas, who was standing outside the company office. Carriages and omnibuses were lined up, waiting for passengers to disembark.

Fifteen minutes later, the Britannia docked.

Ebenezer was one of the first off, followed by dozens of Irish emigrants. He headed towards us, looking tired and drawn.

"Welcome back, father. How was the journey?"

"Tiring as usual. The ship was packed, as you can see. I spent most of my time in my cabin."

"How are my family? Are they well?" I asked.

"Yes, your sisters are fine and your parents are in good health. My wife took them all shopping recently for new clothes. You probably wouldn't recognise them if you saw them."

"How are things in Cork? Is it as bad as they say?"

"It's horrendous. The soup kitchens are swamped with people begging for poor quality soup. People are dying in overcrowded hovels, and more arrive every day.

Many are emigrating to places like Britain, United States, Canada and Australia, depending on what they can afford."

I told him about the relief committee and their plans.

"That's good. I'll have to look into it and see how I can help."

"I'm afraid I have some bad news for you, Father. Mick Murphy was murdered outside his tavern the night before last."

He looked at her in shock.

"My god! What happened?"

She told him about the two men involved and their relationship with Charles Smithers.

"I can't believe it. We should have done something about him a long time ago."

"There's a Wake at Patrick and Rebecca's house," I said.

"I'll go later and pay my respects."

"Did you receive my letter?" asked Phineas.

"Yes, I did. So, Mary's retiring?"

"Yes, we plan on moving into my house as soon as you find a replacement. I have a family in mind who would be ideal."

Phineas told him about Tim and Aoife's circumstances and how they were living at Patrick's.

"Sounds good to me. I'd like to meet them first, though," said Ebenezer.

"If you're going to Patrick's later, you'll probably see them. I'll get my brother to introduce you." I said.

The three of us left Phineas to his work and boarded our carriage.

Ten minutes later, we arrived at the house on Beacon Hill and were greeted by Agnes, the housekeeper.

"Welcome back, Mr Foley. Would you like some tea?"

"Yes please, and could you ask one of the staff to prepare a bath?"

"It's already underway, Sir."

A few minutes later, she placed a small tray of tea on an occasional table in the parlour. I was amazed at the size of the room. It was far bigger than it looked from the outside.

"By the time you finish your tea, your bath will be ready. Is there anything else?"

"No, that'll be fine, Agnes."

As we sipped, there was a knock on the front door. Kath got up to answer it.

"It's probably the porters with my luggage," said Ebenezer.

This is my chance, I thought.

I put my cup down nervously and asked the question:

"I know this is an inopportune time, but I have something I need to ask you."

Ebenezer looked at me and frowned.

"What is it?" he asked, perplexed.

"I'd like to have your daughter's hand in marriage."

"Of course, my boy! What took you so long?"

"I've been waiting for the right time."

"There's never a right time. Life is for living, not waiting."

I explained to him the details of my comical proposal and how I ended up flat on my face. He laughed until he was red in the face.

"I'm delighted, Sean. My wife and I will be proud to have you as part of our family."

Kath returned and looked at her father. He limped towards her and hugged her tightly.

"Congratulations, Kathleen. Have you thought of a date?"

"We haven't discussed it properly, but I was

thinking of mid-May. I'd like to get married here in Boston. Perhaps we can have both of our families here for it."

"Why not? Your mother's coming here in the spring, anyway. Perhaps they can travel together. I'll pay for everything, seeing as you're our only daughter."

"What do you think, Sean?" asked Kath.

"They'd love it, especially my sisters. The furthest they've been is Cork."

"I'm going to freshen up and change out of these clothes. I think I'll pay my respects to Carolina and Rebecca."

"We'll go with you," said Kath.

While Ebenezer was changing, we discussed the wedding.

"You'll have to write to your parents and explain things to them," said Kath.

"I will. Maybe they can stay at Patrick's and spend some time with their grandson?"

"I think your brother and Rebecca would love that."

Chapter 23

Patrick answered the door and invited us in. We entered the parlour and saw the open coffin on the table. Patrick poured us a whisky, then Ebenezer made a toast:

"Gone, but not forgotten. Rest in peace, Mick."

Later on, we followed Patrick into the morning room. Carolina and Rebecca were sitting there with James and Teresa.

"My condolences to you all. If there's anything I can do at this tragic time, please let me know," said Ebenezer.

"You can help us by doing something about that evil man before he ruins somebody else's life," said Carolina, angrily.

"We will, I promise you. We'll have a meeting in a few weeks to discuss it."

We all nodded our heads in agreement.

I took Patrick to one side and told him about Mary retiring and the possibility of Tim and his family running the boarding house.

"That's a great idea," he said.

"Ebenezer would like to meet them first before deciding."

"I'll make the introductions before he leaves. They're upstairs with the children."

"There's one more thing. Kathleen and I are getting married in May. I proposed to her on Finns Farm. It didn't seem right to tell you yesterday after what happened."

"That's wonderful news, Sean. I'll tell Rebecca when everyone's gone."

"Kathleen wants our family to be here for it."

"That would be amazing, and they'll get to meet their grandson, at last."

"Do you think they'll be able to stay with you?"

"Yes, of course. If all goes well, we'll have more room by then."

Ebenezer met Tim and his family and both parties were pleased with the outcome. They agreed to start at the boarding house in two weeks' time.

For the next three days, we had a wake to remember. Patrons of Murphy's Tavern, friends, acquaintances and neighbours, stopped by to pay their respects.

It was an environment of tears, laughter and memories. We exchanged anecdotes and raised our glasses in tribute to a remarkable man.

Thursday 25th February 1847

On the day of the funeral, people arrived from all over Boston. I'd never seen such an assemblage of classes in one place: the elite dressed in all their refinement, the middle classes in their smart but inexpensive clothes and the poor dressed in rags. They were all there to mourn one of the cities upstanding citizen's.

Although Mick wasn't a particularly religious person, Carolina had requested a minister to perform a short service at the house. When he arrived, she presented him with a pair of customary mourning gloves.

She also had a mourning ring made for her grandson and gave it to Patrick for safekeeping.

The pallbearers, myself included, carried the coffin out of the house feet first and headed to the Central Burying Ground on Boston Common. The rest of the cortège followed behind with their heads bowed in respect.

We saw many people stopping in their tracks or turning around as we walked towards Boylston Street. It was deemed bad luck to walk towards a funeral cortège. One could either change direction or stop and hold on to a button.

When he was laid to rest, we returned to the house and drank until the early hours. More anecdotes were told, and we all grieved in our own way.

Thursday 18th March

Three weeks later, on a pleasant spring evening, we were all sat around the dining table at Ebenezer's.

There were ten of us in total: Ebenezer, Patrick, Rebecca, Carolina, Phineas, Mary, James, Teresa, Kathleen and myself.

The maid served us a chicken salad that we washed down with white wine. It was an ample meal for the time of day, and our spirits were high.

Charles tapped his glass with a spoon and asked for order.

"Thank you all for coming. You know why we're here, and that's to sort out the Charles Smithers problem once and for all.

The whereabouts of the two men who murdered Mick remain a mystery. I expect little help from the night watch, but the police are trying their best.

However, I have spoken to Ira Gibbons, the city marshal. He has contacts in other areas and has promised to spread the word. He's circulated a description of the two men, and I believe it's only a matter of time before they're caught.

In the meantime, I suggest we deal with Charles Smithers ourselves. Is there anything you want to add, Carolina?"

"Yes, I want justice for Mick's death, but I don't want anyone getting into trouble. Mick wouldn't want us ending up in jail."

"What are your plans regarding the tavern?" asked Phineas.

"I've signed the deeds over to Patrick. He's going to freshen the place up and put someone in there to manage it.

I'm moving in with them. That way, Rebecca can work, and I can spend more time with my grandson."

"Have you got someone in mind, Patrick?" asked Phineas.

"No, I'm keeping it empty for now. I'd rather

wait until we sort this business out," he replied.

"Has anyone got a plan?" asked Ebenezer.

Teresa stood up and spoke: "James and I have been giving it some thought. We need to use his covetous nature against him. We know he wants to own Murphy's Tavern, and he'll do anything to acquire it.

His own tavern isn't doing very well at the moment because a lot of the locals have boycotted the place. They all know what he's done and what he's capable of. He's surviving at the moment on his inheritance.

The one weakness we can exploit is his addiction to gambling. He thinks he's invincible at the card table which is a dangerous attribute to have especially if you're playing against a professional."

"You want to take him on at gambling?" asked Ebenezer in surprise.

"Not me personally. My husband, James," she replied.

We all looked at each other in astonishment. It was the last thing we expected. We all knew of her strong aversion to gambling.

"Are you sure?" asked Patrick.

"Of course I am. As long as he's not using our money, I don't mind."

"Do you think you can beat him, James?" asked Carolina.

"Yes, I do. I'd need to play against him a few times and get to know his style. You can tell a lot about a player by his habits and facial expressions. It's a science if you know what you're looking for. I'll know straight away if he's cheating. My father taught me every trick in the book.

I think Patrick and Sean should come with me. Let him get used to seeing us together. I'd lose for the first few weeks and lull him into a false sense of security. On the big day, I'd pretend to be short of money and ask Patrick to back me. We'd lose a few hands, then go in for the kill."

"The thing is, I don't particularly want his tavern. Why would I want another one? I'd rather have his land in Ireland," said Patrick.

"That shouldn't be a problem if it's done right," said Teresa.

"What do you mean?" asked Patrick.

"During the game, he's going to ask you to put the deeds of Murphy's Tavern on the table.

You can refuse unless he reciprocates with his land and property in Ireland."

"What do you think, Carolina? Would you risk it?" asked Ebenezer.

"That's a question for Patrick and Rebecca. If it was up to me, I wouldn't hesitate."

Patrick and Rebecca nodded to each other.

"Yes, we'll do it," they said together.

"Does anyone have anything to add?" asked Ebenezer.

"What about the property laws in Ireland? We need to make sure things are legal and abiding," said Kathleen.

"Leave that with me," said Ebenezer. I'll speak to my lawyers. They're a big firm run by two brothers. The oldest, John, runs the office here in Boston while his brother, Mathew, runs their office in Cork. They're both very knowledgeable about these things. They can check whether the land has a mortgage against it, etc. With Patrick being a Protestant, I don't envisage any problems."

"Maybe it would be a good idea if your lawyer was with us on the day to witness things. I could tell Charles that he's sorting out some paperwork for me regarding Murphy's Tavern," said Patrick.

"That's a good idea. I'll arrange it," said Ebenezer.

"When should we do it?" asked James.

"I think we should wait a while. He'll be expecting us to retaliate straight away, but revenge is a dish best served cold. I think the 30th of April would be good," said Teresa.

"That sounds fine to me," said Patrick.

"And me," said Kath. "It will be all sorted before Sean and I get married."

"Have you set a date then?" asked Rebecca.

"Yes, Monday the 17th of May and you're all invited," said Kath.

"We haven't decided on a year yet, though," said Sean drily.

Kathleen gave Sean a friendly punch on the arm while everyone around the table burst into laughter.

At the end of the evening, we all raised a glass

to the success of our plan.

Chapter 24

Wednesday 03rd March 1847

Six days later, Patrick, James and I met up at the office in Broad Street. We'd agreed to meet there before our first visit to the Warren Tavern.

We were nervous, which was understandable. We didn't know what sort of reception we'd get or if he'd even serve us.

A few days before, Patrick had arranged for a sign to be put up outside Murphy's Tavern announcing him as the new owner. He knew that word would get back to Charles Smithers through the grapevine.

We took the omnibus over the Charles River Bridge and got off in Pleasant Street, Charlestown, directly opposite the tavern.

James looked up at the sign that hung above the doorway.

"This was one of the first buildings constructed after the British burned down Charlestown during the war. It's named after Doctor Joseph Warren, who died in the battle of Bunker Hill. He was the one who sent Paul Revere and William Dawes on their messenger rides to Lexington," he said.

"I see you've been doing your homework," I said.

"I'm a mine of useless information," replied James, laughing.

"When we're finished here, we should go to the

Navy Yard to see the Jamestown. It's only a few minutes away. Perhaps there'll be some news about Captain Forbes's proposal."

"Let's keep our fingers crossed. There'll be a lot of work to do if it is," I replied.

We entered a room that was like its proprietor, totally devoid of character. A dust encrusted painting of Doctor Joseph Warren took pride of place behind the bar surrounded by shelves laden with cobwebs. A dozen tables were spaced out around the room, their surfaces covered in ring marks. Charles Smithers was sitting at one of them, playing cards with three other men.

He looked us up and down, recognition dawning in his eyes.

"To what do I owe the pleasure?" he asked, sardonically.

"We're desperate for a drink, and there's nowhere else open in the area," replied Patrick.

"What about your own place?"

"It won't be open for a while yet. I'll be putting someone in there to manage it soon."

"You're welcome here anytime, as was your father-in-law. Have they found the men responsible for his death?"

"Not yet, but they will," said Patrick.

"We've just started a game of poker. Would you like to join us?"

"My brother and I don't gamble. What about you, James? Do you want to play?" asked Patrick.

"I haven't got time today. Maybe next time?"

"Next time it is, then. I shall look forward to it."

"What's your poison?" asked the barman, who had numerous chins and ears that stuck out like a carriage with the doors open.

We ordered a glass of rum each which seemed the safest option and leaned against the bar.

An elderly man entered and asked Charles for a donation towards the relief committee.

"You're the third one I've had in this morning! Piss off out! What have the Irish ever done for me?" he yelled.

"All his wealth originates in Ireland. He wouldn't have this place without it," whispered James, grinding his teeth together in anger.

"Stay calm, don't let him get to you," I replied.

A few minutes later, we finished our drinks and turned to leave.

"I'll see you soon, gentlemen! Have a good day!" yelled Charles from across the room.

"Same to you!" yelled Patrick in reply.

"That's the scruffiest shit hole I've ever been in," I said.

"He gives me the creeps. I can't wait to teach him a lesson," said James.

"You'll have to be patient and draw him in," said Patrick.

"Don't worry. I've got two months to do that. I'll know his game inside out by then. I've already learnt a lot, and we were only there for a few minutes."

"What do you mean?" I asked.

"They're playing with twenty cards because there are only four of them. They have five cards each, and the best hand wins. There's not so much skill involved with that kind of game.

When I play with them, it will be a fifty-two card deck because there'll be five of us, and we'll be able to draw cards. There's a lot more skill involved then.

Did you notice the guy with the beard? The one they called Robert? When he was bluffing, he kept scratching his ear, and Charles was dealing cards from the bottom of the deck."

"I'd never have spotted that," I replied.

When we reached the Navy Yard, we saw several ships in various states of repair. Carpenters, rope makers, block-makers, caulkers and ship riggers were all busy applying their trade.

As we neared the three-masted sloop of war, I recognised Captain Robert Forbes, who was yelling out orders to a group of men who were gathered around him.

"I want everything done as quickly as possible! Time is of the essence, gentlemen!" he yelled.

The men scurried off to carry out their duties and left the captain on his own.

"Good day, Captain Forbes," I said.

"Good day. You're Phineas's friends if memory serves. We met in the Atwood and Bacon Oyster House?"

"Yes, that's correct. Any news from Congress?"

"Yes, some good news at last. They've authorised the use of the Jamestown and the Macedonian to carry food to Scotland and Ireland. The Macedonian will depart from New York and the Jamestown from here. It's the first time that navy ships had been placed into civilian hands.

I'm here to supervise the refitting. We should be able to remove all but two of its cannon with a bit of luck."

"When do you plan to depart?" asked Patrick.

"On the 28th of March, which doesn't give us much time. The relief committee and the local newspapers are swinging into action. There'll be an article in the papers tomorrow requesting a volunteer crew. It's been a frustrating wait, but at least now we'll be able to pay our debt back to Ireland."

"What do you mean?" I asked.

"Nearly two hundred years ago, in 1676, the people of New England were trying to recover from the King Phillips War. Thousand were starving like they are in Ireland now. The Irish sent a ship loaded with supplies. It was a godsend and saved many lives."

"I didn't know that. It's all the more reason to make this work. We have some men available for manual work if you need them. Let us know. We have an office on Broad Street," I said.

"Thank you. I'll keep that in mind. I have to go because there's work to be done."

We said farewell and headed back to the office.

For the next few weeks, Boston was a hive of activity. The response from people in towns and villages across New England was phenomenal.

In a matter of days, funds and supplies poured in. The railroads agreed to ship produce to Boston for free, wharf proprietors donated the use of their docks, and Captain Forbes found his volunteer crew.

Ebenezer's organisational skills and contacts in the Boston community proved invaluable, but what impressed me the most was seeing Irish born Catholics and Boston Protestants working in harmony.

The relief committee raised $150.000 from donors stretching from Arkansas to Maine. Children donated pennies, churches had collections and even the recently arrived Irish Catholics, poor as they were, brought sacks of flour and potatoes to the docks to feed relatives back home.

In the space of two weeks, the warehouses along the harbour were full, and the supplies were ready for loading.

17th March 1847

On St. Patrick's Day, Patrick and I, along with a dozen of our employees, joined up with the Labourers Aid Society to begin the onerous task of loading provisions onto the Jamestown.

For the next ten days, we worked continuously, despite inclement weather. By the 27th March, under Captain Forbes's supervision, we'd loaded 8000 barrels of flour, cornmeal, rye, Indian corn, beans, 400 barrels of port, 100 tierces of ham, mutton, pork, apples, peas, clothes and other supplies onto the Jamestown. Eight hundred tons totalling $40,038.

When we'd finished, we celebrated with a glass of rum with the rest of the volunteers.

28ᵗʰ *March 1847*

The day of departure eventually arrived. Patrick and I were at the Charlestown Navy Yard, watching with interest.

Mayor Josiah Quincy and the relief committee were there, along with thousands of well-wishers that lined up along the shoreline.

"I didn't expect this many people," said Patrick.

"Neither did I, but you can still hear the captain's voice above them all."

He was standing on the quarterdeck, bellowing out orders to his crew.

With its rigging and sails set to take advantage of a northwest wind, the Jamestown along with its 49 volunteers departed to an uproarious cheer from the crowd. Both its flags were unfurled and fluttered proudly in the wind. One was a Stars and Stripes, and the other a white flag sporting a green shamrock.

"I doubt if we'll see them for a couple of

months," said Patrick.

"Probably after the wedding, which reminds me, Kath is meeting up with Rebecca and Teresa later to discuss it. They're going to the Old North Church to ask Reverend John Woart if he'll perform the service at Ebenezer's house."

"I'm sure he will. He's a very accommodating fellow."

"We'd better go. James will be on his way to the Warren Tavern. I don't want him playing without us there for support. I wonder if he's nervous?"

"I doubt it. I think a part of him is looking forward to it," said Patrick.

We met up with James on Pleasant Street. Patrick gave him some money to gamble with, and we entered the tavern. We ordered a rum each and sat at one of the tables in the corner.

Charles was sitting at the next table, heavily involved in a game. The pot was a substantial amount, and you could feel the tension in the room.

He looked at us, acknowledging our presence.

James ignored the game and acted indifferently.

"The girls were at the shop earlier. Teresa was showing them a selection of materials for the wedding dress. I think she'll go for white like Queen Victoria wore at her wedding," he said.

"I'm glad I'm not involved. I wouldn't have a clue," I replied.

A few minutes later, Charles won the pot of money and said, "Would you like to join us, James?"

"Yes, but only for a few hands. I haven't played for a long time, so I'm a bit rusty," he replied.

My brother and I watched with interest, but we didn't have a clue what was going on.

During the game, Charles tried to up the ante from a dollar to two dollars, but James refused. Everyone around the table had to agree for this to happen. After an hour, James dropped out, having lost more than he had won. He stood up and thanked everyone around the table.

"Until next time," said Charles.

It was a nice day, so we walked back. The streets were full of recently emigrated Irish, and the numbers were increasing every day. A young boy, no older than seven, with two candles of snot running from his button nose, came running towards me.

"Any spare cents, Sir?" he asked.

As difficult as it was, I ignored him. We'd have been overwhelmed within minutes if I'd given him something.

"Did you learn much from that, James?" asked Patrick.

"Yes, I did. They're a bunch of amateurs. Charles is in cahoots with the bearded man called Robert. They were signalling to each other, so they knew each other's cards. Charles was dealing from the bottom like last time, and on one occasion, he switched the deck."

"What does that mean?" I asked.

"He swapped the cards for another pack, one that was stacked. That way he could deal himself a good hand."

"My god! I never saw that," I said.

"It helps when you know what you're looking for."

Chapter 25

For the next few weeks, we continued to frequent the Warren Tavern. Charles grew in confidence thinking his cheating had gone unnoticed. James continued in the same way, winning the occasional game so as not to raise suspicion. By the third week, James knew all the signals exchanged between Charles and Robert and their significance.

On the eve of the big day, Ebenezer called another meeting at his house. He had some news he wanted to share with everyone.

Thursday 29th April 1847

The ten of us were sitting around the dining table, waiting with bated breath for Ebenezer's news:

"Thank you all for coming. I've asked you here because last night I received a message from a marshal in New York City.

This marshal has spoken to a Mr Ephraim Bump, proprietor of the Bump Tavern in New York.

Apparently, two trouble makers have been frequenting his place. He's thrown them out on several occasions for fighting, but he's worried that things will escalate to weapons if nothing is done. Both men have a tattoo of an anchor on their right hand."

"That's got to be them," yelled Kath. "When are they arresting them?"

"The marshal and a few of the Municipal Police are going to the tavern this evening. If all goes well, they'll be in Boston Jail by late afternoon tomorrow. They'll probably give evidence against Charles for a lesser sentence."

"That's good news, but what will happen to Charles?" asked Carolina.

They'll arrest him tomorrow evening. As the instigator, he'll probably hang."

"Good enough for the bastard," said Carolina.

"I've spoken to Boston's marshal, Ira Gibbons, and she's keeping me appraised of the situation. If they're early for some reason, I'll try to delay them."

"With a bit of luck, the game will be over by five," said James.

"I've spoken to my lawyer, John Long, and he's going to meet you at the Broad Street office at one. I've explained everything to him, so he's fully aware of the situation," said Ebenezer.

There wasn't much else left to say, so we ended the meeting. Patrick and Rebecca invited Kath and me back to their house. They had something important they wanted to discuss.

The four of us were sitting in the parlour with a glass of wine.

"What is it, Patrick?" I asked.

"Rebecca and I have been thinking. If all goes well tomorrow, we'd like you and Kath to have the land and property in Ireland. You could sign your share of the security business over to us. Don't feel obligated. It's only a suggestion."

Kath and I looked at each other in disbelief.

"But the land in Ireland is worth a lot more than the business here," I said.

"Maybe it was at one time, but since the famine, prices have dropped drastically. A lot of landowners are in trouble because they have no tenants to pay the rent. Many are re-mortgaging just to survive."

"That's true," said Kath. "Things have to change in Ireland for landowners and tenants alike. Plots of land need to be larger, so farmers can diversify. Growing potatoes is not enough on its own."

"What do you think then, Kath?" I asked.

"I'm up for it if you are. I have a small inheritance that my grandfather left me. It's not a fortune, but it'll be working capital for the first few years at least."

I raised my eyes in surprise and said: "I didn't know about that."

"I was keeping it for a rainy day."

"Then we're all agreed. I suggest we celebrate tomorrow once we have the deeds in our hands," said Rebecca.

Friday 30ᵗʰ April 1847

The following day at 12:30, we all met up at the office on Broad Street. Everyone had declared a day off work, and a feeling of nervousness hung over the room.

Carolina and Mary made tea whilst the rest of us stood around chatting.

"Are you nervous, James?" asked Phineas.

"Just a little, which is a good thing. It'll keep me on my toes."

"Sean was telling me about your life in New Orleans and about what happened to your father."

"Yes, I had a strange upbringing, to say the least. Maybe today will make it all worthwhile."

John Long arrived at one and introduced himself. He was a small middle-aged man with straggly grey hair and a tonsured crown. A pair of oval spectacles balanced precariously on the end of his nose.

Patrick told him about our arrangement and that the deeds to the land and property in Ireland should be put in my name.

"That's not a problem. I'm just hoping you can teach Charles Smithers a lesson. He's been involved in a litany of crimes since his arrival in the city, but no one can ever prove anything. I knew the previous owner of the Warren Tavern. He left Boston a broken man after Charles hoodwinked him out of his property."

"Shall we take the omnibus?" I asked.

"There's no need. My carriage is outside," replied John.

The four of us boarded to words of encouragement from the others.

"Be confident and trust your instincts," said Teresa.

"As soon as it's done, head back here. We'll be waiting," said Kath.

Ten minutes later, we arrived at the Warren Tavern. We ordered drinks and sat at a table next to Charles's quartet of reprobates.

"Good afternoon, gentlemen. I thought you'd be drinking at your own place by now," he said.

"We will be soon. This is my lawyer John Long. We've just been going over the contract for the new manager. He should be in there by next week," said Patrick.

"Are you playing today, James?" he asked.

"Yes, of course."

He dragged his chair over to their table and placed it strategically, so he had a good view of both Charles and Robert.

While they played, we pretended to talk business. John took the deeds to the tavern from his briefcase and pretended to explain a clause to us. Out of the corner of my eye, I could see Charles glancing over with interest.

As the afternoon progressed, Charles raised the ante to two dollars. James agreed reluctantly after pressure from the other players.

At four pm, things got intense. The pot had

built up to a sizeable amount. Charles and James were the only two left in. The rest had folded. James had a good hand of four jacks and an ace but very little money in front of him. He knew that Charles had four queens and an ace by the subtle hand signals they'd exchanged across the table.

"Are you betting?" asked Charles.

"I've got a good hand but not enough money to call you. I think I'll fold," said James.

"Wait!" yelled Patrick. "I'll cover the bet if you split your winnings with me. Half of something is better than half of nothing."

"Are you sure?" asked James.

"Yes, as long as Charles doesn't mind."

"Not at all. Your money is as good as anyone else's."

Charles knew he had the top hand. The only hands that could beat him were four aces or four kings. He had an ace in his hand, so he could rule that out. Robert had a pair of kings before he folded, so he could rule that out too.

Patrick threw two dollars into the pot, then James laid his hand down on the table for us all to see.

Charles grinned as he laid his four queens down and dragged the pot towards him.

"Unlucky gentlemen. Another game?"

"Just one more. I want to win my money back," said Patrick.

"Well, why don't we make it a no limit game? You can afford it," said Charles, shuffling the cards.

James noticed him switch the deck as he placed the cards on the table.

"I don't know. What do you think, Patrick?"

"I'm up for it if you are," he replied.

"I'm up for it, as long as I can shuffle the cards one more time for luck," said James.

Charles frowned as James picked the cards up and shuffled them. He then handed them back to Charles, ready for dealing. The stacked cards were now useless.

The betting increased as the game went on, with everyone drawing cards. Charles drew last and dealt himself a queen from the bottom of the deck.

Two of them folded, leaving Charles, Robert and James still in.

Robert had a full house, two aces and three nines. He knew Charles had a better hand, but he stayed in for as long as possible, just for show.

After the next round of bets, only Charles and James remained in.

Charles had four queens for the second time in a row, accompanied by a jack. He knew four aces couldn't beat him because Robert had two of them. There was only one hand that could beat him, and that was four kings. The odds were in his favour. It was unlikely that James would have them from a total of fifty-two cards.

"Why don't we make this a bit more interesting? My tavern against yours, winner takes all," said Charles.

James took a sharp intake of breath and stayed silent.

"Why the hell would I want another tavern? I've already got one!" yelled Patrick.

"Well, it's either that or fold," said Charles.

"He's right," said James. "He said no limit at the start. If you fold, you'd lose what you've gambled so far."

"This is crazy! I don't want another tavern!" yelled Patrick.

"What about your land and property in Ireland? It's not worth what it used to be since the famine, but it's worth something," said James.

"Yes, I can do that if Patrick agrees," said Charles.

"It's fine with me," said Patrick.

John Long had been quiet up to this point but he raised his hand and said, "I hope you don't mind me interfering, but do you have the deeds in your possession? Both sets should be on the table for both parties to see, and any relevant paper-work should be signed in accordance with the law. I have some documents in my briefcase that will validate your agreement."

Charles nodded and yelled instructions to the barman who opened a safe behind the bar and brought over the deeds.

With all the relevant documents signed, witnessed and placed in the pot, the game resumed.

"Let's see what you've got then, Charles," said

James.

"There's only one hand that can beat me, and that's four kings."

He laid his four queens and a jack on the table and grinned snidely.

"Actually, there are two hands that could beat you: four kings or four aces. But you knew Robert had two aces didn't you, Charles?" said James.

They both stared each other in the eye for a few seconds, then James made the hand signal for an ace.

"You've known all along!" yelled Charles, angrily.

"Of course I have. You've been using the same signals for weeks."

James laid four kings and an ace down on the table.

Charles's face went white.

"You bastard! You've been playing me from the beginning!"

"You were the one that was cheating, not me," said James, picking up the deeds.

"Charles Smithers! You're under arrest for the murder of Michael Murphy!" came a loud voice from the doorway.

We all turned and saw Ira Gibbons walking towards us, accompanied by four police officers.

Two of the officers grabbed hold of Charles by the arms and dragged him from his chair.

"This is an outrage! You can't arrest me without proof!"

"Save you complaints for the judge, Mr Smithers. You'll be seeing him in the morning," replied Ira.

As they led him away, Ebenezer limped into the bar and joined us.

"Is it done?" he asked.

"Yes," replied James.

"Thank God for that. They wanted to come earlier, but I delayed them. When you left, I went to the jail to see if there was any news. The two men were arrested last night and transferred here early this morning. They admitted to their crime and blamed Charles for everything."

"Well done, Ebenezer. I think we'd better head back to the office to let the others know. No doubt they'll be anxious and waiting for news," I said.

"Yes, I think a celebration is on the cards if you'll excuse the pun," said James, laughing.

Chapter 26

We entered the office with expressionless faces. They all looked at us with concern.

"What happened?" asked Kath, frowning.

"We've done it! The land is ours, and Charles has been arrested!" yelled James with delight.

Everyone started dancing around the room in excitement. Even our lawyer joined in.

"Well done, gentlemen! This calls for a celebration!" yelled Phineas, excitedly.

Carolina hugged James and Teresa tightly.

"Thank you, both. Mick will be looking down on us with a smile on his face," she said.

"Let's go to the Oyster House! The drinks are on me!" I yelled.

We were there in minutes. Patrick organised one of the larger tables in the corner, so we could all sit together. I ordered oysters for everyone, plus two bottles of champagne. Kath and John Long were sitting on either side of me.

"Thanks for everything today, John. We appreciate it," I said.

"The pleasure was all mine, I can assure you. It was so good to see that man having his comeuppance."

"How long do you think it will be before we can move into the property in Ireland?" I asked.

"I'll be sending all the paperwork to my brother in Cork on Monday. He'll register the property in your name and take care of everything.

It should take about six weeks, maybe less.

An agent has been looking after the land for Charles since his grandfather's death. Mathew, my brother, will speak to them and make sure the property is looked after until your arrival. The current staff will be kept on to keep things ticking over. When you get there, you can decide who you want to hire and fire.

You'll also need to close your bank account here in Boston and open a new one in Cork. We can sort that out for you and transfer any balance. When are you thinking of travelling back?"

"What do you think, Kath?" I asked.

"Your family are arriving next Friday. They've booked their return for the 29th of May. We could travel back with them and stay at my father's house in Cork for a few days."

"That's a good idea," I replied.

"If that's the case, you should be in Cork around the 16th of June. That gives them plenty of time. Do you know where the office is in Cork?"

"Yes, It's on St. Patrick's Street near my father's drapery. I've been there before."

"Good, I'll make sure the accounts are available for your perusal."

The waiter arrived with the champagne and placed both bottles on the table. I poured and invited Carolina to make a toast.

"To Mick, justice and new beginnings!" she yelled.

We raised our glasses aloft and repeated her

words.

We continued our celebration late into the night, ending up at Ebenezer's house to sample his vast collection of whisky. The rest is a blur and remains so to this day.

Friday 07ᵗʰ May 1847

A week later, the Britannia arrived.

Rebecca and Kath were nervous about meeting our parents for the first time.

"I wonder what they'll say when they find out we're moving back to Ireland?" asked Kath.

"They'll be surprised, especially when they find out we own the Big House and the land that comes with it," I replied.

"I can't wait to see their faces. When will you tell them?"

"When they're sitting down at Patrick's."

"Do you think you'll recognise your sisters? It's been at least five years since you've seen them."

"I think so."

Patrick and I were scanning the crowd, looking for a familiar face, when a young girl tugged at my arm.

"Sean?" she asked.

"Who are you?"

"I'm your sister, Cathy."

My brother and I looked at each other in shock.

"My God! Look at the size of you! You're a young woman!" I yelled.

"Well, I am nearly sixteen," she replied.

We both gave her a big hug and introduced her to everyone.

"Where's the rest of them?" I asked.

"They're with Ebenezer's family. They'll be here soon. Da sent me ahead."

I looked up and saw my mother trundling along the gangplank, holding my father's arm for dear life. My other sisters were trailing behind, followed by Ebenezer's family.

"There they are!" I yelled.

"I'll get them," said Cathy.

"I'll come with you. Our carriage is ready and waiting. I'll see you all tomorrow," said Ebenezer.

My mother was an emotional wreck when she picked her grandson up for the first time. My father had a tear in his eye and waited patiently for his turn.

We introduced Kath and Rebecca.

"I'm so glad my sons are happy," she said, emotionally. "You don't know what it means to us."

We had a group hug while young Patrick clung to his father's leg, desperate to join in the proceedings.

I organised two carriages, and we were soon on our way.

Carolina was standing on the doorstep when we arrived. Patrick introduced her to our parents, and they exchanged courtesies.

"Did you give them my address as I told you to

in my letter, Da?" asked Patrick.

"Yes, I did," he replied.

"Then your luggage should arrive shortly."

We all sat in the dining room while Carolina made tea. My father sat his grandson on his knee while my mother looked on adoringly.

"How was the journey, Da?" I asked.

"Not as bad as I expected. We were lucky with the weather. We all had seasickness at some point apart from Cathy who was like a seasoned sailor."

"How are things in Cork?" asked Patrick.

"Pretty dismal. Men, women and children are dying in their thousands. I've never seen such penury. It's even worse in Skibbereen and the countryside. Your mother and I count our blessings every day. If it wasn't for Ebenezer, God knows where we'd be."

"Were you there when the Jamestown arrived?" I asked.

"Yes, it was amazing. It arrived on the 12th of April. Thousands of people lined the hillsides and wharves, cheering wildly. The dignitaries were all there, and a band played Yankee Doodle. I just hope that more ships will follow in their wake."

"I'm sure they will, Da. Relief committees are being set up all over America," said Patrick.

"Is everything set for the wedding, Kathleen?" asked my mother.

"Yes, Rose. The service will be at my parent's house, and the wedding breakfast will at the newly opened Revere House Hotel on Bowdoin Square.

It's nearby, only a few minutes walk.

My friend, Teresa, who you'll meet at some point, has made my dress. She and her husband own a drapery store."

"Patrick mentioned them in one of his letters," said my mother.

"The girls will have to be measured tomorrow for their bridesmaid's dresses."

"Oh yes, they're very excited. They haven't stopped talking about it since we left Cork. What colour is your dress?"

"It's white, similar to what Queen Victoria wore at her wedding. The girls will also be in white. It seems to be the style at the moment."

"It must be a stressful time for your parents with so much to do."

"It certainly is. My father is going to send the invitations out today, and my mother's going to be busy putting together a Bridal Trousseau."

"What's that?"

"It's a collection of items a bride needs during her married life. Sewing implements, petticoats, linens, shawls, handkerchiefs, slippers, hair combs and brushes, things like that. There's an emporium on Washington Street that she wants to visit."

"My God! That'll be a small fortune."

"It will be, but it's tradition and something my mother wants to do."

"Where are you going to live once you're married?" asked my father.

Kath and I looked at each other knowingly.

"I think it's time you told them," she said.

"Told us what?" asked my mother, intrigued.

"When you return to Ireland on the 29th of May, we'll be coming with you. We're moving back there permanently," I said.

They were both at a loss for words.

I explained the events of the last few months, from Mick Murphy's murder to the poker game at the Warren Tavern, and the arrangement that Patrick and I had made.

"So, you now own the Big House?" said my father in disbelief.

"Yes, we do."

"You were right, Son, and I was wrong."

"What do you mean?"

"On the day of Rebecca's funeral, we stopped outside it. Do you remember?"

"Yes, I do."

"I said we'd never own property like that in my lifetime, and you said, never say never. I didn't know what you meant. You said nothing is impossible and that anything can happen. You certainly proved that."

"What do you think, Ma?" I asked.

"I'm dumbstruck. It's the last thing I expected."

"What happened to that horrible man, Charles Smithers?" asked my father.

"He was found guilty. They hung him yesterday at Leverett Street Jail."

"Well, at least that's justice for Carolina and Rebecca. It won't bring Michael back, but it's something."

Kathleen and I finished our tea and said goodnight. They were all tired and in desperate need of sleep.

I walked Kath home, and we discussed the wedding on our way.

"You're going to need a few new trunks if you want to take your Bridal Trousseau to Ireland with you," I said.

"Yes, I think Teresa and James sell them. We'll have a look tomorrow when we take the girls."

"I'm going to need one myself. The one that I brought to Boston with me five years ago, fell apart."

I kissed her goodnight on the doorstep and arranged a time for the morning.

Chapter 27

Saturday 08ᵗʰ May 1847

The following day, I arrived as Kath's brothers, John and George, were leaving. John was now 23 and his brother 18. They both shook my hand vigorously and apologised for rushing off.

"We're both meeting friends we haven't seen for a while," said John.

"Don't worry, we'll have time to talk at the wedding," I replied.

Agnes showed me into the parlour. Ebenezer and his wife were sitting on two comfortable armchairs in front of an unlit fireplace. A mahogany pianoforte stood in the corner, and a beautiful landscape by John Constable hung above it.

They both rose and greeted me.

"It's so nice to see you again. Did you sleep well after your journey?" I asked.

"Like the proverbial log. It felt so good to sleep in a proper bed and be able to stretch one's legs out without knocking something over," said Ebenezer.

"I know what you mean. There's not much room in those cabins. Even the rats are hunchbacked."

They both laughed as I pulled up a chair to join them.

"Did you manage to write the invitations?" I asked.

"Yes, It didn't take me long. It'll be just family, and a few close friends," replied Ebenezer.

"I heard a rumour that the town hall has set up a committee to deal with the Irish emigrants. Is that true?" I asked.

"Yes, it is. There are thousands arriving every day, but it's not the volume that's the problem. It's the malignant diseases like ship fever and cholera that they bring with them. The cities institutes are overwhelmed so they've had to do something."

"What are they planning?"

"They're turning Deer Island into a quarantine station. They've already started building a hospital there. A Dr Joseph Moriarty will supervise things with a team of fifty doctors, nurses and support staff. Many people will die, but they have to protect the rest of the population."

"It's not surprising that so many are sick. The conditions they're travelling under are beyond belief. I saw a ship arrive recently that was barely seaworthy. Its steerage was packed so tight with men, women and children, that they could hardly move."

"Yes, It's a difficult situation. I wish there was more we could do."

Kathleen walked in looking elegant in a turkey red calico dress with ruffled sleeves and a matching bonnet.

"You're looking very soigné today, Kath," I said.

"Merci, Monsieur. I didn't know you spoke

French."

"Only a few words," I replied.

"We'd better go. Your sisters will be waiting."

They were standing on the doorstep when we arrived, all dressed and ready to go. My parents were just about to leave.

"Where are you going, Ma?" I asked.

"We're taking young Patrick for a walk."

"Are we walking?" asked my youngest sister, Mary.

"Yes, it's not far," replied Kath.

We took a shortcut across the common, and Kath told them a little about the history. They were fascinated, especially when she told them about the Hanging Tree. Fifteen minutes later, we arrived at the store on Federal Street.

The shop looked as inviting as ever with its beautifully proportioned arch windows and its portieres entranceway. A large unit stood to the right displaying notions: needles, threads, buttons and skeins of yarn.

Bespoke shelving, containing bolts of cotton, linen, stunning silks and luxurious damasks, lined the wall on the left.

I was surprised to find my brother at the store. He was talking conspiratorially to James and had that look of devilment in his eyes that I was familiar with.

"I know that look. What are you up to?" I asked.

"Nothing, I'm just here for my final fitting and

to make sure everything is going to plan. I'm your groomsman, a responsibility I take seriously."

"He's right, Sean. Everything is as it should be. It's just the bridesmaids' dresses to do. Teresa and her seamstresses will work on them over the next few days. It's been a busy time for us. We've another wedding to prepare for on the same day," said James.

Kath introduced my sisters to Teresa, who led them to a fitting room at the side of the store.

"You're all much taller than I thought, but that won't be a problem," she said.

She went to work with her tape, measuring their bust, waist and hips.

"When will they be ready?" asked Kath.

"On Wednesday. Can you bring them back then for a final fitting?"

"Certainly. There's something else I wanted to ask you. Sean and I are going to need some steamer trunks for our journey to Ireland. Do you sell them?"

"Yes, we do. They're in a separate room at the back. James knows more about them than I do. James! Can you show Kath and Sean the steamer trunks while I measure these young ladies!"

"Yes, Dear!" he replied.

We entered the room and were immediately hit by the olfactory odours of leather and wood.

"We have a wide selection. Some are domed on the top and others are flat. Personally, I think the flat ones are better for storage.

This one has been a best seller of ours and ideal for both of you. It's finished in leather and waterproofed with tree sap. All the fittings are brass and designed to stand the ravages of an ocean journey. It also has a false bottom where you can keep your prized possessions. It's better to be safe than sorry. I can have your initials engraved on it if you like?"

"That would be nice. I think one would be sufficient for me and maybe three for Kath?"

"Two will be enough for me. I already have one large trunk," said Kath.

"Could we have them delivered? One to Hawkins Street and the others to Kathleen's?"

"Yes, no problem. They'll be with you by the end of the week."

We spent the rest of the day showing my sisters around the city. We visited Quincy Market and Faneuil Hall then stopped off for food at the Atwood and Bacon Oyster House.

On the way home, my sister Cathy bought herself a book at the Old Corner Bookstore on School Street. It was called The Raven and written by a local author named Edgar Allan Poe.

"I've read that. It's about a grieving lover and a Raven that visits him. It's got a very supernatural atmosphere," said Kath.

"I shall look forward to reading it," replied Cathy.

Kathleen devoted the next week to my family. They spent two nights together at Finns Farm in

Concord, an experience my sisters will never forget. They got on well with Luke, John and Michael and spent most of their time exploring the countryside on horseback.

I spent most of that week with my brother. I signed the business over to him and made sure everything was in place for a smooth transition.

The days passed quickly, and before I knew it, the eve of our wedding arrived. I went to bed that night full of nervous anticipation, eventually falling asleep in the early hours.

Monday 17th May 1847

I woke up at seven, feeling famished. Aoife made me a light breakfast of eggs and toast.

"You won't need much this morning, Sean. You'll be having a big meal after the wedding," she said.

Tim and Aoife had thrived since taking over the boarding house. They were in their element and loved every minute of it.

"This is fine, but I'll have some more coffee if I can."

"I'll bring you some shortly. What time is the ceremony?"

"It's at eleven. I'll have a bath here before I go. My brother and I will dress at Kathleen's, seeing as our wedding clothes are there."

"I'll get Tim to prepare a bath for you."

I arrived at Kathleen's in plenty of time and

was greeted by Agnes:

"Good morning, Sean. Everyone's upstairs getting ready. Your brother's in the end room on the right."

"Thank you, and good morning to you," I replied, cordially.

The entire house looked amazing. A profusion of flowers filled every corner, and extra lighting had been placed in the parlour to brighten the area.

I entered the room upstairs to find my brother making a final adjustment to his cravat.

"Good morning," he said. "I was here early, so I thought I'd dress."

"The house looks amazing. I think Agnes and the staff have been busy," I said.

"Yes, they've done a good job. Our sisters are here. They're helping Kathleen with her dress."

"I'd better get ready. I don't want to be late for my own wedding."

"There's plenty of time," said Patrick.

My brother and I had identical suits: a high collared shirt tied with a cravat, a ruby red embroidered waistcoat, black pantaloons, black silk stockings, dress boots, white kid gloves, and a black dress coat faced with white satin. The rest of the men in attendance dressed similarly but with less flamboyancy.

I made short work of dressing and had everything on apart from the dress coat. My brother handed me the ring, and I placed it in my waistcoat pocket.

I put on the dress coat and soon realised that something was amiss.

"The arms are too short! He's given me the wrong coat!" I screamed. "Kath is going to kill me if I wear this!"

"Oh my God! James said they had another wedding planned for today. Perhaps he got them mixed up."

"What am I going to do? I'll be a laughing-stock."

Patrick laughed until tears ran down his face. He walked to the wardrobe and reached in for another coat.

"This one's yours," he said, sputtering with laughter.

"You bastard! You switched them."

"I'm sorry. I couldn't resist it."

"I knew you were up to something when we visited James and Teresa's store. You had that look on your face."

Eventually, I saw the funny side of it, and we walked downstairs together in fits of laughter.

All the guests had arrived on time and were gathered around the punch bowl. Phineas handed us a tumbler each.

"Have a glass of liquid courage. It'll settle the nerves," he said.

Ebenezer and Anne joined us and commented on how dashing we looked. I told them what Patrick had done with the dress coat. They found it hilarious and nearly choked on their punch.

As I filled my glass, I heard a knock at the door.

"That will be Reverend Woart. I'd better let him in," said my brother.

Patrick introduced him to everyone and obtained the certificate of marriage.

A few minutes later, Agnes approached me and whispered in my ear: "They're ready when you are."

I walked to the top of the stairs, and the sight that beheld me will stay in my memory forever.

Kathleen looked stunning in a long white satin dress with a Honiton lace overskirt. Her veil was made of Brussel's lace and attached to an artificial wreath of orange blooms. On her feet, she wore silk white slippers decorated with ribbons. In her left hand, she grasped an embroidered white handkerchief with our initials sewn in.

My sisters looked just as elegant in plain white dresses that reached the floor. Their veils were shorter than Kath's, as was the custom.

The girls led the way while Kath and I followed behind.

We stopped in front of the parlour window. The bridesmaids stood to Kath's right, and my brother to my left.

Once everyone was in place, the ceremony began. After a few words and prayers from the Reverend, we exchanged vows. I placed the gold ring, engraved with our initials, onto the fourth finger of Kathleen's left hand and kissed her on the cheek. Reverend Woart pronounced us husband and wife, and the festivities began.

Chapter 28

Although the Revere House Hotel was only a ten-minute walk away, Ebenezer had arranged carriages for everyone in case of inclement weather.

Kath and I were the last to arrive, and we were welcomed by the guests who were gathered around the Corinthian columned entranceway.

Paran Stevens, the proprietor, welcomed us to the 220 room hotel and led us inside. Its interior looked magnificent with a marble lobby floor, costly furniture and elegant drapery. I could see why it had the reputation of being the most prestigious hotel in Boston.

A small function room had been prepared for us where we were served a lavish meal, starting with a lobster salad with a border of aspic.

After that, we had a choice of several dishes: Chicken fricassee, salmis of duck, beef a la mode, pigs feet, calf feet jelly, oysters in a variety of ways, baked beans with pork, and curried lobster.

After the meal, there were speeches followed by a soloist playing the pianoforte. A great time was had by all. We danced until late into the evening, eventually heading home at eleven.

Tuesday 18th May 1847

The following morning, Agnes served us breakfast in bed and coffee served in fine bone china.

"I could get used to this," I said.

"Make the most of it. We won't be living like this on the farm. We'll be up with the birds every day," said Kath.

"I know, and I'm looking forward to it. I love the sound of birdsong in the morning. It makes you glad to be alive."

After breakfast, we joined Anne and Ebenezer in the parlour. The room was back to normal with no evidence of the preceding day's festivities.

"Good morning, Mrs MacCarthy," said Anne, smiling.

"Good morning, Mother. That sounds so strange."

"And what have you got planned for today?" asked Ebenezer.

"We're meeting my brother this morning to formulate a plan for the farm. I value his opinion. He's got one of the most analytical brains I've ever seen, and his knack for predicting future trends is remarkable," I said.

"That's wise. You've only got eleven days until you depart. I've been giving it some thought. I think you should take as much non perishable food back with you as possible. It'll be cheaper here and more accessible," said Ebenezer.

"I was thinking the same myself," said Kath.

"You can leave that side of it to me if you like. I've got the right contacts, and we can store it in our warehouse until departure."

"Thanks, Father. Let us know the cost, and

we'll repay you."

We said farewell and walked out into the sunshine. It was a cloudless day without a breath of wind.

My parents were just leaving when we got to Patrick's. My mother looked proud as she pushed the perambulator.

"Off to the common, are you?" asked Kath.

"Yes, we're making the most of the weather," replied Rose.

"Where are the girls, Ma?" I asked.

"Gone shopping with Carolina."

We entered the house and joined my brother and Rebecca in the parlour.

"I've got some news for you. I've sold the tavern," said Patrick.

"You have? Why?" I asked.

"I'm going to invest in the railways, both here and in Britain. It's something I've been thinking about for a while. It could have a massive effect on your future's too."

"What do you mean?" I asked.

"There are going to be new routes in Britain over the coming years. At the moment, there are four major ports, Bristol, Glasgow, Liverpool and London, but as the railways expand, more will open up, and live cattle exports from Ireland will increase tenfold.

It depends on whether you want to survive or thrive. If you use the bulk of your land for grazing, you'll thrive.

Grow vegetables and grain by all means, but stay away from the potato for a while. It could be a few years before the blight disappears completely."

"There's something else you have to consider," said Rebecca. "The population of Ireland is decreasing every day through death and migration. I know that sounds indurate, but there are going to be fewer mouths to feed in the future."

"That's very true and something to bear in mind," replied Kath.

"I was thinking of employing more labourers to work the farm as opposed to tenant farmers. They could live at the Big House initially while we build new accommodation for them," I said.

"That's a good idea," said my brother.

Patrick and Rebecca were going to the office to meet with a client. We walked with them to the corner of Broad Street then went our separate ways.

"Shall we go to the Oyster House?" asked Kath.

"Yes, I'm going to miss going there. I've developed quite a taste for oysters."

"There are a few places in Cork that sell them. There's one near the English Market that's supposed to be good. We could always go there if you get a craving."

When we arrived, we found Captain Robert Forbes and his brother John sitting at the bar. They both rose when they saw us.

"Ah, Sean! I hear congratulations are in order,"

said Robert.

"Thank you. I didn't know you were back."

"We arrived yesterday."

I introduced Kathleen, and they both kissed her hand.

"We know your father well," said John.

"Who doesn't?" said Kath, laughing.

We ordered oysters and Guinness and sat down next to them.

"How was the journey, Robert?" I asked.

"It was the most frightening I've ever experienced. We had the foulest weather exacerbated by an inexperienced crew. It lasted for six continuous days, and at one point, I didn't think we were going to make it.

When we got there, we had a great welcome. They invited us to a sumptuous feast which was a bit embarrassing considering the number of people dying on the streets.

Eventually, we got the food out to where it belonged, but it took far longer than it should have.

I wanted to see the suffering first hand, so Father Mathew, a local temperance priest, showed me around the city. I was completely overwhelmed, and the sights I beheld will haunt me forever."

"Do you think you'll return with another ship?" I asked.

"I hope so. I'm going to speak to the relief committee this week. The overall mission was a success, marred only by the loss of a man overboard on the return journey. Ironically, he was the only Irish born crew member."

"That's so sad," said Kath.

I told them about our plans to move back to Cork.

"You'll have to prepare yourselves mentally. You'll want to help everyone, but it's impossible."

We sat there for an hour discussing an array of subjects. John spoke about Samuel Morse, and the effects telegraphy was having on the country while his brother spoke knowledgeably about the Mexican and American War. He was convinced it would be over within the year.

I could see Kath was getting bored, so we made our excuses and left for home.

"Can we go back via Hawkins Street? I need to pick up some clothes," I said.

"Why not? You should move everything over to our house. Tim and Aoife will be eager to rent the room out."

"I'll do it today if my new steamer trunk has been delivered."

We arrived to find Aoife scrubbing the doorstep.

"Good morning. I'm surprised to see you two out of bed," she said, winking.

"Good morning," we both replied.

"Did a trunk arrive for me this morning?" I asked.

"Yes, it did. Tim took it up to your room."

"Wonderful. I'll be moving to Kath's once I've

packed, so the room will be available to rent."

"That's great. Call me when you're done, and Tim will help you carry it down."

It didn't take us long. I placed my prized possessions under the false bottom while Kath, who was more experienced than me, packed my clothes in an orderly fashion.

"Most of these things can stay in the trunk until we depart. I can wash the rest closer to the time," she said.

Tim and I carried it down and placed it in the hallway.

"I'll get a carter to drop it off later."

"Thanks, Tim. It's much appreciated."

"I hear you're moving back to Cork. Will you say hello to Father Sullivan for me and tell him we're safe and well?"

"I will, Tim, no problem."

When we got home, Kath started going through her own things, deciding what to keep and what to throw. By the end of the week, she had three large steamer trunks full to the brim.

Our last days in Boston were both happy and sad. We visited everyone we knew, promising to return for a holiday in the future.

Saturday 29th May 1847

The day of departure finally arrived. We boarded the Britannia to shouts and cheers from our family and friends that lined up along the wharf. We both had tears in our eyes as we waved from the deck.

I'd been living in Boston for over five years, and a lump formed in my throat as I thought of the people I'd met during that time.

The hardest part was saying goodbye to my brother. We'd always been there for each other through thick and thin. Life without him by my side would take some getting used to.

My parents and sisters were standing beside us, waving frantically. My mother sobbed uncontrollably, and my father fought hard to fight back the tears. They'd spent every day with their grandson, and to see them like this was heart wrenching.

"There's only one thing for it. We'll have to provide them with a grandchild," said Kath, seriously.

"It'll be a tough job. Have you seen the size on them berths?"

"They are small, but it'll be fun trying," she replied with a glow in her cheeks.

We stayed on deck until the wharf disappeared from sight, then a member of the crew showed us to our cabin.

Much to my relief, the journey to Cork was uneventful. I'd been expecting the worse, but the weather had been perfect apart from one day when we were confined to our cabin.

Kath spent most of her time in the ladies saloon with my mother and sisters while I kept my father company in the dining saloon. I asked him if he wanted to move in with us at the farm, but he declined. He said they were happy working for Ebenezer, and my sisters loved living in the city.

Chapter 29

Wednesday 16th June 1847

We arrived in Cork as scheduled. We disembarked and were immediately submerged in a deluge of skin and bone. Children and adults alike clung to us, begging pitifully for food. Captain John Hewitt had warned us of this, but to see it up close was disconcerting.

Eugene appeared from nowhere and whisked my parents and sisters away.

"You'll have to get a Jingle. There's no room for all of you!" he yelled.

A Jingle is a type of carriage, peculiar only to Cork. We managed to get one and soon caught up with Eugene. We travelled in silence, both of us were too upset to speak.

When we arrived, Eugene handed the keys of the house to my father.

"Can you pick us up at nine in the morning Eugene? We have to meet with Mathew Long to sort out some business," said Kath.

"Certainly. Ebenezer informed me in his letter. I believe you're now the owners of the Manor House."

"That's correct. We'll need you to take us there tomorrow, after our meeting. Have you got a carriage big enough to carry us and five steamer trunks?"

"I have a long coach that I bought off Bianconi

Coaches. It will be more than big enough. I'll bring someone with me to help. You'll need the extra protection when you get into the city. People are desperate and desperate people do desperate things."

"Thanks, Eugene. We'll see you in the morning," I said.

It wasn't long before my parents got the house in order. My mother prepared a meal while my father and I organised baths for everyone. We retired early, looking forward to the luxury of a feather bed.

Thursday 17th June 1847

The following morning at nine, Eugene and an associate of his named Shamus, turned up at our door. They both had pistols in their belts.

"Are the weapons really necessary?" I asked.

"I'm afraid so. It's not safe on the roads these days," replied Eugene.

Twenty minutes later, we arrived at the office in St. Patrick's Street. Mathew Long and his secretary were just opening the doors for the day. He recognised Kathleen immediately and welcomed us warmly.

"I've been expecting you. If you could take a seat, I'll go through everything with you," he said.

Two hours later, we left the office feeling buoyant. The farm was in a far better state than we expected. The proceeds from a recent shipment of livestock had been paid into my new account in Cork, giving us a healthy balance.

We left Cork and saw very little until we stopped at Clonakilty for dinner. Famished people flocked around us, begging for food. A woman carrying a dead child asked us for money for a coffin.

"It's like this wherever you go. It's even worse in Skibbereen. Dead bodies lay abandoned on the sides of the roads, and disease is rife," said Eugene.

We witnessed this ourselves as we neared our destination. We saw people carrying bodies wrapped in Calico and others heading towards the workhouse in the hope of shelter.

"Stop the coach!" I yelled suddenly.

"What is it, Sean?" asked Kath.

"I just saw someone I know. A very dear friend of my mother's."

I hopped down and approached her. She had a boy at her side who was about fifteen years of age. They were both emaciated like all the others we'd seen. She hugged her son close and looked at me warily.

"What is it?" she said.

"It's me, Mrs Ryan. Sean MacCarthy. We used to be neighbours."

"Sean! I thought you were in Boston."

"I was, but I now own the Big House. It's a long story. Where are you going, Patricia?"

"To the workhouse if we're lucky enough to get in."

"Where's your husband and the rest of your children?"

"They're all dead. It's just the two of us now."

"I'm sorry to hear that. Would you like to come with us? We can offer you work and a roof over your head."

They both looked at me in shock.

"Yes, please. I'd cry with happiness if I had any tears left," she said.

"Thank you, Mr McCarthy. You don't know what it means to us," said Francis, her son.

"It's the least I can do. You were always kind to us when we lived in the clachan."

I helped them aboard and introduced them to Kathleen.

When we arrived at the gates to the Big House, we found three armed guards blocking our way.

"I'm Sean MacCarthy, the new owner!" I yelled.

They opened the gates hurriedly and let us in.

"Welcome to your new home, Mr MacCarthy. I'm Daniel O'Connor, manager of the estate. We were expecting you yesterday. Sorry about the frosty reception, but we've had people trying to break in."

"That's fine," I replied.

Eugene guided the coach along a winding drive and reined in the horses at the entrance to the house.

We climbed down and were met by an elderly woman in a maid's uniform.

"I'm Sarah, the housekeeper. The staff are all lined up inside waiting to meet you," she said.

I introduced her to everyone and explained Patricia and her son's circumstances.

"I'll make sure they're attended to immediately. You look a bit like your mother. I remember her working here as a maid. She was a hard worker and a scholar. When Charles's son George had lessons, I always made sure your mother was sitting in. She had a wonderful capacity for learning."

"She taught my brother and me, so we have a lot to thank you for."

We entered the house into a flagstone hallway. The maids and kitchen staff lined up on either side, perfectly attired in crisp clean uniforms. Sarah made the introductions, then gave us a brief tour of the house. An hour later, we were sitting in the library sipping tea.

"I think we should call a meeting, Sean. We should start as we mean to go on," said Kath.

"I agree, and there's no time like the present."

We spent the rest of the day in discussions with Daniel O'Connor and several of the senior farmhands.

We told them of our plans to employ more people and what our aims were for the future. They agreed wholeheartedly and came up with some novel ideas of their own.

We worked hard for the next few years. We took on labourers from the workhouse and increased our exports.

Most of our profit went back into the farm. We improved the living conditions for our employees and prepared large tracts of land for grazing.

We also grew far more vegetables than needed and gave the surplus to the soup kitchens.

By 1849, the farm was well established. The demand for exports had increased as my brother had predicted.

Ireland itself was still in the grip of the famine despite Westminster declaring it over. Poverty and starvation were common, and cholera raised its ugly head again.

On Aug 03rd of that year, our first child Victoria was born. We named her in honour of the Queen who was visiting Cork on that day.

Our second and last child Sean was born on July 10th 1852. The famine was over by then, apart from a few isolated places.

My story now comes to its end. I could go on and tell you about my children and the events that shaped their lives, but that seems unfair. It's their story, and it's for them to tell.

Chapter 30

Bourton on the Water

02nd November 2019

Sean nearly jumped out of his skin when the alarm went off. He pressed snooze, buried his head under the quilt and tried to get back into the very pleasant dream he was having.

A few seconds later, the high-pitched tone of his mother's voice echoed through the house.

"Sean! Breakfast will be ready in 20 minutes!"

His mother could summon the devil when she wanted to.

He jumped out of bed, grabbed his little bag of toiletries and headed for the hallway bathroom.

After seeing to his ablutions, he dressed, picked up the book and went downstairs.

His father, Brendan, was sitting at the dining table nursing a mug of tea while his mother was busy applying the finishing touches to a full English breakfast.

He sat down and placed the book on the table.

"Did you finish it, Son?"

"Yes, Dad. I couldn't put it down. I read until four in the morning. Did you know that our whole existence is based on an act of kindness by my five times great grandfather and his brother back in 1841?"

"No, I didn't. I'll have to read it."

Sylvia placed their breakfast's in front of them and sat down to eat her own.

"The mini skip has arrived, Sean. I bagged all the rubbish up earlier so it won't take us long to fill it," said Brendan.

"That's fine. We'll crack on with it after breakfast."

Feeling sated, they went out into the garden to make a start. Brendan sat down on a garden bench to put his boots on while Sean looked up at the grey skies above.

"It looks like rain," he said.

"Not surprising for this time of year," replied his father.

As they worked, Sean gave his father a brief outline of the book, starting with Rebecca's tragic death. He told him about Boz, the journey to America, the famine in Ireland and the poker game in Charlestown. His father listened keenly, enthralled with the story.

They made short work of filling the skip, and within the hour, they were back in the kitchen drinking tea.

Sean continued with the story, but as he neared the end, he jumped out of his seat in alarm.

"What's wrong?" asked Brendan.

"I've just realised something. When Sean moved back to Ireland in 1847, he had a brand new trunk."

"That's probably the one that's upstairs."

"It is. It fits the description perfectly," said Sean.

"So, what's the big deal?"

"In the story, it had a false bottom where he kept his valuables. There might be something hidden in there."

"Well, you'd better look," said Brendan.

Sean flew up the stairs, opened the hatch and pulled the sliding staircase down. Within seconds, he was kneeling next to the trunk. The lid was open from the day before. He leaned in and removed the rest of the documents, carefully placing them in a pile next to him. With the trunk now empty, he removed the false bottom. It came away easily to reveal a small compartment. In it sat a brown paper parcel.

He removed the outer packaging nervously. If this was what he thought it was, it could be worth a small fortune. He sighed with relief when he saw the perfectly preserved book. He opened it and found the following words on the title page.

To,
 Sean MacCarthy
    from
        Your Esteemed Friend,
            Boz.

He took it downstairs and showed it to his parents. Their mouths fell open when they saw it.

"Do you think it could be worth anything,

Dad?"

"Who knows? It could be. There's an antique dealer I know who goes to the Mousetrap Inn. His name's Gary Rimmer, and he owns Rimmer's Antiques in Broadway. He only lives around the corner. Do you want me to ring him?"

"Yes, please, Dad."

Twenty minutes later, Brendan got off the phone, smiling from ear to ear.

"He doesn't believe me and insists on seeing it for himself. He's on his way."

A few minutes later, there was a knock on the door. Brendan showed him in and introduced Sean.

Gary was in his early sixties and of average height. He had grizzled hair to the nape of his neck and a meticulously groomed beard.

"I hear you have a very interesting book to show me," he said.

"I have," replied Sean.

Gary donned a pair of white gloves and took the book off him.

He sat down at the dining table and studied it in silence. After a few minutes, he spoke.

"Your father said there was a story involved, written by one of your ancestor's."

"It's on the table by the side of you. It mentions the book."

"That's wonderful provenance. I think you have something of value here. Do you wish to sell it?"

"Yes, I think so."

"Then I suggest a specialist sale at Sotheby's. I can make an appointment for you if you like. I have a few contacts there."

"That sounds good. I live in London, so it's no problem for me."

"They'll do some research first and value it. They'll also guide you through the entire auction process. It's worth checking out their website. It's very informative, and it will give you an insight into the inner workings of an auction house. I'll ring you when I've made the appointment."

"That's perfect, Gary, and thank you for your help."

"Your welcome. I'd wish you luck, but I don't think you're going to need it."

The following week, Sean attended a meeting at Sotheby's. After meticulous research, they authenticated the book and entered it into a specialist auction on the 27th of November.

A frantic few weeks followed. Sotheby's regional representatives throughout the world wove their magic, and before long, his story was spread across the front pages of every newspaper in the world.

27th November 2019

On the day of the auction, Sean woke up with butterflies in his stomach. After a shower, he put on his best suit, had a quick cup of tea and caught the underground train to Sotheby's Auction House in the heart of London's Mayfair district.

Snow was forecast, and a cold wind blew down New Bond Street, chilling him to the bone. He entered the building, glad to escape the cold.

"Good morning, Mr MacCarthy. It's nice to see you again." said the young receptionist.

He'd met her on his previous visit when a member of staff had given him a tour of the building.

"I'm a bit early, so I thought I'd have some breakfast in the restaurant upstairs."

"Why not? I can recommend the scrambled eggs with truffle. It's a breakfast to die for."

"That sounds nice. I'll give it a go."

"You've got an hour before the auction starts, so you've plenty of time."

On the way, he had a quick look around the exhibition area and found his lot on display in a glass cabinet in the corner. It seemed to be generating quite a lot of interest as people jostled to get a better look. One guy, who Sean thought was American because of his black Stetson and ornate leather boots, seemed entranced as he leaned in for a closer look.

He eventually arrived at the restaurant and took a seat in the corner, next to a window overlooking the street. His stomach rumbled as the heady scent of truffle emanated from the kitchen.

This is impressive, he thought as he took in his surroundings. It had been tastefully decorated in the contemporary style with vibrant colours throughout. Subtle music played in the background, adding to the ambience.

A good looking waitress approached him holding a menu.

"Good morning, Mr MacCarthy," she said with a smile.

"Good morning," he replied. "How do you know my name?"

"I think everyone knows who you are. You've been in all the newspapers. I think your story has captured the imagination of everyone."

"I know what I want. I'll have a flat white and some scrambled eggs with truffle please."

"An excellent choice. I'll bring your coffee straight away."

While he waited, he took a catalogue out of his inside pocket. It contained factual information about the lots for sale at today's auction. He found his and read it for the umpteenth time. It described it perfectly, including its provenance.

As he flicked through the pages, a piece of paper fell to the floor with his handwriting on. He picked it up and began to read. It was a glossary of terms used in auctioneering that he'd copied down the previous day from the Sotheby's website.

He was known in their world as the consignor or the seller in layman's terms. It also explained a lot about the online bidding service (BID now) and how some people could bid without even being there (absentee bids). He'd underlined two words at the bottom: Fair Warning. It would be the last call made by the auctioneer, giving the bidders one last chance to bid before the hammer came crashing down.

His breakfast didn't disappoint. The flavour of truffle and scrambled eggs was sublime and left him wanting more.

He paid his bill using his credit card, hoping he had enough balance to cover the cost. Much to his relief, the card was accepted, and he made his way to the saleroom.

It was packed. Every seat was taken apart from one. A high desk ran the full length of the room on the right-hand side, armed with telephonists waiting for phone bids.

A woman approached him dressed in a smart grey suit and a white blouse.

"Good morning, Mr MacCarthy. My name's Colleen, and I'm the Saleroom Manager. I've kept a seat for you in the corner where you'll have a good perspective of the room. You'll be able to see and hear the bids as they come in."

"Thank you, Colleen. I can't get over how many people recognise me."

"Well, you have been on the front page of every newspaper in the country," she replied, laughing.

She showed him to his seat and wished him luck.

The sale began dead on time when a charismatic auctioneer addressed the room.

There were several items up for sale before his,

which gave him a chance to get into the flow.

When his turn came, his stomach flipped, and an eerie silence fell over the room.

The auctioneer held it up in his gloved hands for everyone to see and described it.

"And now ladies and gentlemen. It's time for the pièce de résistance.

This was originally published as a serial in the English literary magazine called Bentley's Miscellany from 1837 to 1839. It was released as a three volume book in 1838 and is the author's second novel.

As you can see, it's in pristine condition, which considering its age is remarkable. It's also signed by the author as follows:

To,
 Sean MacCarthy
   from
     Your Esteemed Friend,
         Boz.

This in itself is unusual as the author rarely signed books using his nickname. The title page contains the following:

OLIVER TWIST

OR THE

PARISH BOY'S PROGRESS

BY BOZ.

However, Boz is more affectionately known as Charles Dickens. Has anyone ever heard of him?"

There was a titter of laughter around the room that immediately disappeared when the bidding started.

They came flying in from all quarters, but the experienced auctioneer stayed calm and soon had them dwindled down to a mere handful.

A phone bidder had taken the bidding up to £220,000, and everyone was waiting for a response. Nothing happened for several seconds, then the auctioneer spoke:

"Any more bids ladies and gentlemen! Fair warning!"

Sean held his breath in nervous anticipation. *I can pay off all my debts and still have plenty over,* he thought.

Before the hammer came down, a new bidder raised his paddle. It was the man Sean had seen earlier, wearing a black Stetson and ornate leather boots.

"£240,000 in the room! Anymore bids ladies and gentlemen? Fair warning!"

After a few seconds, the hammer came crashing down, concluding the sale.

"Sold to the gentlemen wearing a Stetson!"

A few seconds later, Colleen approached him and said, "The money will be paid into your account, Sean, minus the commission of course."

"That's great. It will keep the bank manager off my back for a while."

"The man who bought the book would like to meet you. Would you mind?"

"Not at all."

They walked to the other side of the room, and Colleen introduced him. The man was about the same age as Sean and stood at six foot two. He had red hair and piercing blue eyes.

"My name is Patrick MacCarthy. I believe we're related," he said in an American drawl. "My five times great grandfather and your five times great grandfather were brothers.

When I read the article in the paper, I couldn't believe it. It mentioned a story that you found in a steamer trunk, based on the journals of Sean Maccarthy. I knew straight away because our family has a copy. Sean must have sent it to his brother. We've treasured it for many years."

"That's amazing! I'm so glad you bought the book. Are you doing anything now?" asked Sean.

"No, they've got everything they need."

"There's an Irish bar across the road. We should have a drink to celebrate," said Sean.

"That's a good idea. Let's go."

The two distant cousins walked into the bar and ordered Guinness.

"To your esteemed friend, Boz," said Patrick, raising his glass.

"Or Charles Dickens," said Sean, raising his.

Author's Note

I hope you've enjoyed reading this book as much as I've enjoyed writing it. If you have, would mind leaving a review and star rating on Amazon.

Your Esteemed Friend is a work of fiction. All the characters, apart from some well known historical figures, are a product of my imagination.

Printed in Poland
by Amazon Fulfillment
Poland Sp. z o.o., Wrocław

76503762R00148